RESET
A Thriller

PERI PARKS

VENUS BOOKS
Orlando

Published by Venus Books, a division of Venutek, LLC, a Florida limited liability company, P.O. Box 2331, Oviedo, FL 32762

ISBN-10: 0984860916
ISBN-13: 978-0-9848609-1-3

www.periparks.com

Cover art by Jeff Leimbach

This book is dedicated to my family.

CONTENTS

PROLOGUE

The room smelled of chemical. The sources were obvious: new carpeting, fresh paint, new modern-looking worktables, and typical hotel-banquet chairs, though brand new. There were no windows and the lights were dim with the projector illustrating the slides the speaker was sharing. He was an older man with a kind demeanor. His curly hair enweaved gray threads at the temples and his bronze complexion had a ruddy surface. He was somewhat soft spoken, while passionate about the subject. The conference room was filled with 20-somethings occupying every chair.

A woman in front was listening intently. Her large round belly began contorting and she put her hand on it and felt a tiny foot poking through. Her caresses overcame the barrier of shirt and skin to sooth the baby within. She shifted her weight in her chair and swept her long brown waves back behind her ears.

A moment later the snapping and unsnapping of pieces on a toy-circuit board pulled her attention. A handsome boy sat on the untrodden carpeting imposing his will on his toy. He was against the wall at one end of the classroom and his mother was at the desk next to him. The boy resembled his mother.

When they broke for snack, the boy ran out of the classroom to the hallway, where cookies and soft drinks were waiting for them. His mom called out, "Jason, save some for the rest of us!"

Mari eyed the snacks carefully. She grabbed an oatmeal-raisin cookie and a bottle of PowerAde. Jason's mother approached her, "That your first?"

"Yes," Mari glowed.

"Boy or girl?"

"Don't know yet. But it doesn't matter."

"Can you believe all this?" the mom said referring to the class they were taking.

"Our founding has always been an interest of mine. Now," she laid her hand on her belly and let her gaze follow, "it seems more important than ever."

"I'll drink to that," said the mom as she took a swig of her Diet Coke.

"Is he your only child?"

"Yup. He's a genius, too. I can't keep him busy enough. He hears everything and remembers everything he hears. So he'll remember this entire lecture, even though he's building all these electronic circuits. I don't know anything about electronics. But I love to just keep learning, whatever it is. He and I are the same that way," she patted Jason's head as he came to the table for more cookies.

Everyone started moving back into the classroom, so the rest followed. Upon sitting in their seats, the old man resumed his talk:

"A **bill of rights** is a set of the most essential rights of the citizens of a community, usually a country or nation. Bills of rights have been established to prevent governments from infringing on the freedom of the individuals over which they are tasked with governing. The first use of the term "bill of rights" was in 1689 in England.

"The Founders of the U.S. Constitution debated whether to entrench a Bill of Rights into it, since its purpose was merely to define the limits and boundaries of the new Federal government that would provide for the Common Defense of the Many States. During the ratification process of the Constitution ten of twelve proposed amendments were incorporated as the first ten amendments to the Constitution, fixing the unalienable rights of individuals within the Many States of America United to a condition of permanence such that the rights are unalterable by legislation and forever entrenched.

"The Bill of Rights in the U.S. Constitution begins with the premise that the individual is *sovereign*, meaning that the individual's rights are supreme and that individuals are free and autonomous. Governance granted to the States is constituted by the sovereign individuals via State Constitutions. Thus the States are also *sovereign*, being free and autonomous to legislate as they see fit on all matters that do not infringe on individuals, enunciated through the Bill of Rights. Governance is granted by the States to the new Congress limited to the enumerated powers granted to the Congress in Article I, Section 8 of the Constitution. The sovereignty of individuals and States is emphasized and reiterated in the Ninth amendment and as the endpoint of the Tenth amendment. That is, a reader would find a list of the powers granted to Congress within Article I, read through the list of entrenched, unalienable rights of the individuals in the first eight amendments, and then if any question remains, find that **all remaining powers** are the purview of the States to legislate, via the Tenth amendment, if the State so desires, otherwise all other powers remain with individuals".

She looked down on the workbook he had handed out as he paused,

"First Amendment

Congress shall make no law respecting an establishment of religion, or prohibiting the free exercise thereof; or abridging the freedom of speech,

3

or of the press; or the right of the people peaceably to assemble, and to petition the Government for a redress of grievances.

Second Amendment

A well regulated Militia, being necessary to the security of a free State, the right of the people to keep and bear Arms, shall not be infringed.

Third Amendment

No Soldier shall, in time of peace be quartered in any house, without the consent of the Owner, nor in time of war, but in a manner to be prescribed by law.

Fourth Amendment

The right of the people to be secure in their persons, houses, papers, and effects, against unreasonable searches and seizures, shall not be violated, and no Warrants shall issue, but upon probable cause, supported by Oath or affirmation, and particularly describing the place to be searched, and the persons or things to be seized.

Fifth Amendment

No person shall be held to answer for a capital, or otherwise infamous crime, unless on a presentment or indictment of a Grand Jury, except in cases arising in the land or naval forces, or in the Militia, when in actual service in time of War or public danger; nor shall any person be subject for the same offence to be twice put in jeopardy of life or limb; nor shall be compelled in any criminal case to be a witness against himself, nor be deprived of life, liberty, or property, without due process of law; nor shall private property be taken for public use, without just compensation.

Sixth Amendment

In all criminal prosecutions, the accused shall enjoy the right to a speedy and public trial, by an impartial jury of the State and district wherein the crime shall have been committed, which district shall have been previously ascertained by law, and to be informed of the nature and cause of the accusation; to be confronted with the witnesses against him; to have compulsory process for obtaining witnesses in his favor, and to have the Assistance of Counsel for his defense.

Seventh Amendment

In suits at common law, where the value in controversy shall exceed twenty dollars, the right of trial by jury shall be preserved, and no fact tried by a jury, shall be otherwise re-examined in any court of the United States, than according to the rules of the common law.

Eighth Amendment

Excessive bail shall not be required, nor excessive fines imposed, nor cruel and unusual punishments inflicted.

Ninth Amendment

The enumeration in the Constitution, of certain rights, shall not be construed to deny or disparage others retained by the people.

Tenth Amendment

The powers not delegated to the United States by the Constitution, nor prohibited by it to the States, are reserved to the States respectively, or to the people."

She had read them several times before. In her notebook was a list of questions she had previously jotted down from her reading. She knew in Amendment 1 that some of the States had established State religions. But she wondered why the word "Congress" was mentioned only in Amendment 1 and whether they made a mistake about the rest of the rights in the First Amendment. She was eager to ask this man her questions, which were:

1. Did the Founders believe that the States could limit freedom of speech, freedom of the press, and the right to peaceably assemble? Or did they expect these rights to already be enumerated within State Constitutions? Or was Congress only prohibited from establishing a national religion?

She had left a note in her planner to research the State Constitutions that were in existence at that time. As the speaker paused a moment to organize his next point, she recalled that everything changed during the Progressive Era, which ramped up starting about 1880 to new heights in the early to mid 20th century and never really ramped down in modern times.

2. When did the meaning of the First amendment change FROM Congress won't create a Federal religion that all States must abide by TO the current

understanding that all governments cannot participate in any religiosity?

She knew from her studies that the U.S. Supreme Court did *a 180°* during the Progressive Era, too. It had always been that States were sovereign until some court decisions they made, which completely changed the definition of the word, "regulate" in reference to the Commerce Clause. There were many Court decisions in the mid-20th century that completely changed the Constitution.

3.   When did the word "regulate" change FROM its definition then, meaning to keep freely flowing TO its current meaning, which is to make rules that limit free flow? What was that Supreme Court decision that expanded the Commerce Clause to allow Congress to decide how much Commerce a person could engage in within his own State? Who were the Justices in the majority in that case? Who appointed them? Had they expressed their judicial philosophy ahead of time?

She read the Fourth Amendment. And she thought to herself, *this has to be the most abused amendment of all by Governments.*

4.   The Fourth amendment: Brainstorm a list of all violations in current accepted practice to the Fourth amendment, e.g. airport screening to fly commercial jets, DUI checkpoints, the Patriot Act allowing warrantless wiretapping, etc. Find articles on this subject in law library.

She thought for a minute about her long desire to become a lawyer. She and Jake got married young. They lived frugally and saved every dime they could. But they both wanted a big family. There wouldn't be time yet for law school. Not with her first child on the way. She patted her belly again. She went back to the Fifth Amendment next. Perhaps this was the most abused of our rights, more than the Fourth.

5. Look up cases of eminent domain takings of private
    property. Look up Supreme Court cases that
    allowed the taking of private property. Read up on
    IRS code allowing the IRS to impound private
    property. Read up on history of land use
    restrictions, zoning, homeowner associations, and
    the like, which limit the use of private property. Is
    there anything in the State Constitutions to protect
    private property? Read about the use of paycheck
    garnishment by the authorities to pay fines and
    awards.

She knew the term "Militia" meant the people that
assembled to defend their homes and communities. She knew
Ben Franklin had organized militia back in the 1760s when
the People living in rural Pennsylvania were attacked often by
the nearby Indian tribes. Their homes were burned, the
people tortured by scalping, burning, or by being cut over and
over for hours or days. She also knew the French had armed
these Indian tribes and encouraged them to attack the settlers
in rural Pennsylvania. Franklin had worked tirelessly
petitioning Governor Penn to provide a defense force for the
community. Penn refused. Then Franklin petitioned the King
of England to provide a defense force. And he refused. So
Franklin knew that ultimately, it was up to the People to
defend themselves, particularly when their governments
would not. He organized the militia among the men of the
community, had them practice drills, and implement sentries
and warning systems so that the people had time to be ready
for an attack.

The instructor resumed now. She looked up from her
notes and listened intently. He kept teaching them about the
past. She wanted to know what to do in the future. Until then,
she would keep learning.

ONE

A Saturday in November, West Lawn of U.S. Capitol

B rrrr. The cold was penetrating.

Mari moved down the sidewalk among the throngs as she wondered why she was here. She wanted to be heard. She paid good money to be here. She took the time away from her home and family to do her part. She was driven, compelled to be here. To speak, to be heard. But there were no listening ears, no effect from her efforts. Despite the chilly air, the frustration boiled inside her.

J.B. looked out the window toward the west lawn. He felt hopeful for a moment. He was not alone in the struggle to set the world back upright. Mari's senses told her to look so she glanced up at the window. But the window was too distant to see J.B. staring back at her and the crowd.

Looking unfazed by the 45 degree weather, the Capitol Police rode their bicycles in teams around the Capitol Reflecting Pool to make sure there were no disturbances in the crowd. The dispatcher asked one how it was looking. He replied, "This is the nicest crowd we've ever had. No worries."

Later ECF News reported 200,000 people marched along the Washington Mall to the West Lawn. The reporter announced, "We interviewed dozens of people from the crowd. About half of them were wearing shirts with verbiage of different amendments from the Bill of Rights. Congressman Ray Blanzing spoke at the event, dubbed a *Bill of Rights Restoration Assembly* and wore a shirt that read 'The right of the people to be secure in their persons, houses, papers, and effects, against unreasonable searches and seizures, shall not be violated.' The crowd was chanting 'LI-BER-TY' over and over. Meanwhile national socialist counter-protesters numbered in the hundreds gathered near the Botanical Gardens. They held up pre-printed signs heralding the Government's new safety measures. Their placards said 'Keep Us Safe' and their group chanted 'Keep Us Safe' repeatedly. This is Namia Pruvati with ECF News."

Later that day Mari walked to the Metro Station at L'Enfant Plaza and returned to Reagan National Airport by train. There she stripped to her underwear wearing a 4th Amendment T-shirt, and was groped by the TSA agent anyway, perhaps because she went through in her underwear, and then redressed, walked to the gate and sat waiting for her plane to board. In the waiting area she read an article in an aviation magazine she found on a bench that explained the history of air travel security. It was titled, "The Shifting Overton Window of Passenger Air Travel". She knew who Joseph Overton was and to what the "window" referred. It was the spectrum of what was considered *normal* by people within a range of possibilities. Propagandists, educators, and cultural influences can change Overton windows gradually, through small shifts rather than pushing the window completely away from "normal".

"In the United States through the 1960s, passengers needed only a boarding pass to gain passage to their seat on an aircraft, operated by the company with which they contracted for travel by air to their destination. Though there were occasional incidents of lawlessness during air travel from its beginnings, the significance of those events did not capture the public's attention until the late 1960s and early 1970s with ubiquitous television access by the public and the use of film footage to bring the consequences visually to both the public mind and the criminal mind: the former demanding more security and the latter scheming opportunities to exploit.

"Sky-jackings of passenger planes grew in number until they peaked in 1969 at 82, eight of which that year had hijackers demanding passage to Cuba.

"As a result of numerous, widely televised sky-jackings, President Nixon implemented the Federal Sky Marshall program in 1968 with just 6 armed agents. Following a sky-jacking in 1970 by Pakistanis, President Nixon implemented the use of Sky Marshalls on most or all commercial flights.

"The first metal detector for passenger screening began in 1972 because it was becoming too expensive for the Federal Government to man the increasing numbers of flights with Sky Marshalls. Widespread passenger screening with metal detectors began in 1973. At first, there was public outrage at the use of metal detectors because of delays, inconvenience and infringement upon the rights of innocent citizens. Passengers were not guilty of crimes and were protected by the 4th of the Bill of Rights from being searched without cause. While the outrage lasted for some time, eventually the public became accustomed to the new requirements for boarding airplanes. As young people grew up under the new rules, their view was that metal detectors were completely normal and not at all intrusive. Thus their Overton window had shifted in the 1970s and 1980s.

"By the mid-1980s there were thousands of Sky Marshalls. But as metal detector use became universal and safety procedures were greatly expanded, the number of Sky

Marshalls was reduced gradually to just 33 armed agents by 9/11/2001.

"The government has also expanded its power to conduct searches and to prohibit passengers from access to commercial aircraft. For example, after the 1988 Pam Am bombing over Lockerbie, Scotland, luggage had to remain in the possession of passengers

"The 9/11 attacks resulted in draconian and drastic changes in commercial aviation rules, *because the public demanded something be done.* Thus the Overton window shifted dramatically because of the vulnerability people felt. Immediately after the 9/11 attacks, the Sky Marshall program rapidly ramped back up to thousands of armed agents. The Transportation Security Act of 2001 was hurriedly passed by Congress and signed by President George W. Bush. There was no debate over whether the government should seize control of the screening process from the airlines and airports, only whether the screening agents should be federal employees or contractors, depending on which political party was in control and which would be favored by such decisions.

"Additionally, after 9/11 all luggage was to be screened with x-ray devices, procedures were rewritten to handle suicide hijackings, and cockpits were secured with stronger doors, door locks, rules for keeping them closed, and armed pilots. The airports' role in passenger screening had been revoked by an act of Congress, removing their responsibility for passenger screening and transferring that responsibility instead to the Federal government, along with all control. All passenger screening is now standardized across all airports regardless of their size and volume of passengers.

"In the past few years the Transportation Security Administration has granted itself greater powers, broadened its procedures and completely ignored the 4th amendment in a far more expensive, far less effective effort to prevent suicide hijackings. Passengers are no longer subject to mere metal detectors but to invasive body image scans or invasive body searches. While there are pockets of resistance by the public over isolated incidents, overall the public continues to be willing to trade their rights for the sense of security such searches seem to provide.

"Security experts agree: there will be more attacks which will bypass the strongest of efforts to prevent them, just as the most-secure prisons can and are breached occasionally and just as the most secure networks are hacked. Because systems are created by people, they have weaknesses and malicious people will uncover and exploit those weaknesses. The authors wonder what possible shifts could yet be made to passenger travel in response to certain future breaches."

Reading this made her stomach lurch. She fought it off by drinking a swig of her water. She wondered why this article was in a magazine available for passengers to read in the terminal. She tore the article out and put it in her purse. She looked at the jetway door. Just then they called for passengers to begin boarding. She packed up her things, tossed her trash into a bin, and joined the queue to board her flight, suppressing a burp that was destined to come any moment.

Though the take off was smooth, she continued feeling a bit nauseous. She felt doomed. There was no escape. These intrusive and invasive security screenings were here to stay and she felt powerless to stop it. She and thousands of others protest but government officials aren't listening. Her stomach started convulsing. She got out of her seat and walked to the back of the plane so she could vomit in the rest room. As she moved down the aisle, her face in her hands, she heard a low growl. She looked up and a man with dark, wavy hair, green eyes, and olive skin ran toward her, with a pointed object. She realized, too late, she could not get out of his way in time. She saw the cream-colored object, which looked like a knife, slowly coming toward her stomach. She knew it would impact momentarily. Just then her stomach heaved and the contents rushed out of her mouth all over his front side. The knife penetrated her skin. She felt the rip. It took forever to tear across her skin. It burned. She fell to the side. She could feel her face dripping with her own vomit. She heard a thud – that was the back of her head hitting the armrest. Then there were stars and everything went black.

Jake laughed while his kids played tag at the playground. One son ran up behind him to hide from the others. He loved their little faces, giggles, and hugs. He patted the head of his son just before he zoomed away to avoid being tagged by another boy. Jake walked over to the monkey bars where his daughter was climbing. She reached out and touched his short hair, which felt like a brush to her and tickled her hand. Jake encouragingly asked her if she could climb down on her own, since she was getting so high up on the bars. He looked at his watch and decided to end playtime to get Mari from the airport. She had only been gone since yesterday but he missed her anyway.

It was a gorgeous fall day. He knew they made the right move when they came to Florida to raise their children a few years back. They could play outdoors all year long. And their community was everything he wanted: family-oriented with a great church and a pastor who understood the people in his flock.

Jake and Mari decided to have 4 children. They both worked but they met like-minded couples in their church when they arrived 10 years before. They agreed to set up a co-op to provide childcare for their combined children. All 6 parents would take equal turns watching their combined 9 children at their 3 homes. One couple had 2 children and the other couple had 3. They discussed if it would be more fair for the parents with more kids to have more time with all the kids but decided not to because they also had more expenses for school, food, supplies, and later college. Today was

Saturday, however, so Jake had only his children at the park. The co-op agreed not to babysit for each other on weekends. They would rely on family members or teenagers in the neighborhood for non-work days.

Jake rounded up his kids into the van and announced it was time to go to the airport to pick up their mom from her trip to D.C. where she was attending the *Bill of Rights Restoration* march. It took nearly ten minutes to get the kids to make the transition, to climb in their seats, to buckle them up, and to make sure all the gear was stowed. He climbed in himself, started the engine, and headed for the airport.

.

TWO

Saturday Evening, Indian River Lagoon, Florida

The line jiggled. It dipped into the water. There was another tug, this one longer. Jasmine snapped her pole back. She snagged it. She reeled the fish into her kayak. It struggled to cough the hook out of its mouth. Jazz smiled at the pretty little ladyfish. She grabbed it, angled the hook out of its mouth and tossed it back into the Indian River. The sun was setting and the sky was aglow with rose, fuchsia, amber, and teal shades approaching the deep blue clear sky of a fall day in Florida. She felt so alive.

She had a great week. As the top sales director for the Southeast for the largest electronics distributor, she was making tidy sums in commissions. She was only 27 and was already being groomed to be promoted to Vice President of sales at Berk Distributors. She had been making six-figures for the past 4 years. She played as hard as she worked. But she also saved every dime she could. Life was good.

The sky was growing darker by the moment. She pulled out her headlamp and put it on her forehead. She started paddling toward her car on the shore. As she paddled the mullet scurried away from under her boat. They splashed and jumped and surrounded her boat. She enjoyed this time on the water. Comforted by thousands of fish all around her, she was not afraid of the dark, she was not afraid to be kayaking alone in the huge Indian River on a Saturday night.

After she pulled out of the water, she put her kayak on the roof rack, stowed her paddle and life jacket, dropped her shorts and put on dry ones, and climbed into her Honda Pilot. Her phone was buzzing in its cradle. "Jasmine's Phone" lighted the display. She slid the lock release over and answered. It was her brother-in-law, Jake.

"Hey Jake – what's up?"

Heavy breathing. Heaving and part sobs.

"Jake? Jake –what's wrong?"

"It's. It's Mari." More heaving and now heavy crying.

"Jake – take a deep breath. What do you need? Do you need me to come over?"

"Mari is in the hospital. She was stabbed on a flight back from D.C. She's in Atlanta. I need to go to Atlanta."

"What? What are you saying, Jake? Atlanta? Stabbed?"

She listened to her brother-in-law as he tried to regain control of himself. She just waited. She didn't say anything more. She learned this early on working in sales. It was most important to listen. People never talked as fast as you want or expect. It always takes them longer than you think before they say what they really want to say. She waited. She thought about this. What was Mari doing in D.C.? How could she have been stabbed? He needed her to go take care of the kids so he could get to Atlanta to be with Mari. She did some calculations in her head. An hour drive to their place. She'd have to swing by her house to get clothes, computers, and a few other things. It would take her a half hour to get to her house and another half hour to pack up. So it would take her 2 hours. She could be there in 2 hours. She kept waiting until he pulled himself together. She finally said, "I can be there in 2 hours. Do you need me to find you a flight to Atlanta?"

Jake finally stopped making sniffling and heaving sounds. He said, "The airline is waiting for me. They're taking me to Mari. I'm leaving now. Call one of my neighbors and ask them to come over until you can get here." Then he just hung up.

Oh crap. Neighbors? She's never called any of their neighbors. She's only waved from a distance. She opened her iPad and pulled up the map. She typed in her sister's address and found the map view. She then clicked on the neighbor's house and linked the address to the public records database of homeowner names. She grabbed the names and addresses off the screen and pasted them into the Whitepages look up. She found a phone number, clicked it, and her iPad dialed the number on her iPhone.

"Hello?"

"Hi. This is Jasmine Roberts. I'm Mari's sister."

"Yes, Jasmine, hello. Is everything okay?"

"No. Mari is in the hospital in Atlanta. Jake just called me and I'm packing up to go over there to look after their kids. But I can't be there until 2 hours from now. Would you go over and watch over them until I get there?"

"Oh my goodness. Oh my. Uh. Uh. Yes. If I can't I'll get one of the other neighbors to help, too."

"Excellent," said Jasmine. "See you soon."

Next Jasmine called her parents in Ohio to tell them what she knew. They said they'd fly down to Florida to do what they can to help. They figured they'd be on a plane Sunday morning.

Jasmine started the car and drove home. She made a list in her head of what she needed to pack and where she needed to stop on her way there: gas station, bank, drug store, and coffee shop. The sky was jet black now. The stars were sparkling overhead. She started to let the news Jake told her sink in. She shook her head. What was this world coming to when a mother of four is stabbed on an airplane on her way home?

THREE

Saturday Night, U.S. Capitol

J.B. picked up the phone and called his mentor, Congressman Ray Blanzing.

"Ray, it's me, J.B. Saw your speech and the crowd. This is great!"

"Yes, J.B., the People are waking up. It was exhilarating to have such a large crowd of concerned citizens. I have to run. But keep up the good work at your end, too."

J.B. did not seek the spotlight. He really had no aspirations to be a politician or run for Congress. He was a P.E. teacher at an elementary school before he came here. He loved to be silly with the youngsters. P.E. was the favorite subject of most of the children, too. So he was always a popular guy with the kids. But as a schoolteacher, he was forced to join the Teachers Union. And the union leaders were pushing Congress to pass all kinds of laws that should have been handled at the State level. And he saw his own State Legislature pass all kinds of laws that should have been handled locally by the School Board. After 8 years of teaching, he got more involved. First he ran for a union leadership position so he could change these problems locally. Even though he was a teacher and dues-paying member of the union for so many years, he could not get his name on the ballot. The leadership blocked his every attempt. He tried resolving this through his own Principal and his fellow teachers at his school to no avail. Then he enlisted the School Board for help but they wouldn't cross the line. He called his State Representative and State Senator for help, but their reply was that the Union, as a private corporation, made its own rules. Everyone was powerless to change the Union's election process to open a spot on the ballot for his name. He realized then that his teachers union was a scam. They were taking his money and the dues of all the other teachers, not to represent *teachers*, but to use the money and power for their own personal goals, which he did not agree with.

As he complained to the School Board, the state legislators, and finally the news media, he became a well-known person in the community. He had met so many important people, gave so many speeches about the union leadership election process, that he finally got noticed by like-minded members of both political parties' executive committees in his county. One asked him to run for Congress because of his passion, his speech-making skill, his winning personality, and his first hand experience with some of the problems in which power-mongers were taking over Unions to help others push a socialist agenda. His name spread quickly and there was little opposition in his campaigns. He won his election and became a Congressman.

He packed his overnight bag and headed to the train station, where he would be magically transported overnight back to his home. This coming week Congress was out of session, and he had 14 speeches and events to attend. He would be going to 5 different high schools to speak to the students about the Bill of Rights so they would know part of what it means to be an American. But first he had to endure the new procedures at the Amtrak station – where passengers had to strip down, pat down, or be x-rayed to travel. Even him, a member of Congress, was among the untrustworthy traveling public.

Jake's eyes were puffy. His head hurt. His stomach was rattling like a pair of maracas. But at least he was sitting in the plane on his way to Atlanta. The questions were bouncing around his head: How bad was her injury? Why did this happen to Mari? Was anyone else injured? What happened to the guy that stabbed her? What was Mari feeling now? Was she awake or asleep? He was grateful that before she left Friday afternoon that he held her for a long embrace and let her know he was proud of her and supported her. This gave him comfort. Because he thought she might not be safe on this weekend trip. He was right about that. But he was also right to support her.

Every day for the past 5 years Mari lamented to Jake about the downfall of the United States. She worried about their 4 children and the world they'd grow up in. Her hair started graying at her temples despite her being only 32. But she was a history major in college. She was in love with the Founding Fathers. She did her senior research project on the farming operations of George Washington. She had described his many innovations and inventions of the great man himself, like his grist mill, crop-rotation strategies, the seed-laying plow, fertilizer development, and the organization structure for managing his farm. Matteson thus called him "America's first scientific farmer". And his farm was diverse with a variety of crops to extend the growing season and replenish the soil, plus a fish farm that was novel at the time. He kept meticulous records and extensively studied agriculture. Later he was inducted into the American Philosophical Society for his agricultural expertise.

Washington was also quick to discover that the laws the King's parliament was passing in England would soon put him out of business. He could not buy and sell wares as he chose, but only could trade with the King's appointees, whose prices were "mean". He responded by expanding his farm's capabilities to produce as much as possible and by selling to local colonists exclusively. The strict rules he was forced to operate under drove him into mounting debts. As the Intolerable Acts were passed and enforced, Washington was first to see the possibility of having to resort to arms; he was first to see that pleas to Parliament were ineffective and resulted in more rules and enforcers as the Colonists continued to protest. Efforts escalated rather than lessened their predicament. As a member of the Virginia House of Burgesses, he helped lead a boycott of purchasing items that would be taxed, as a means of getting the taxes repealed. He was steadfast in the principle that Parliament may not tax citizens without their consent.

Jake rubbed his eyes while the airplane began its descent. He had to be strong when he got to the hospital. He had to be there for Mari. To reassure her that she would be all right. That she did the right thing by speaking up and marching before the Capitol to restore the Bill of Rights. She could see the trend of events and knew it was away from liberty and toward tyranny. He would be strong, supporting, smiling. For her. Because she was a strong, principled woman. A dedicated mother to their children. A patriot. And the love of his life.

The phone buzzed in her pocket as she finished her sentence on camera. Shaun shut off the camera and Namia pulled the loose strands of silky black hair from her cheek and back into place as she pulled her phone out of her pocket to see what the text message was.

Namia Pruvati was born in the U.S. to parents who emigrated from India. They owned a small motel on the edge of the Virginia town in which she grew up. They were the salt of the earth. They loved America. Namia had her moments, though. Some of the kids were cruel in elementary school because she looked darker and different. Some of the girls in her middle school were jealous because she was a stunning beauty. By high school, though, it all smoothed out. She had boyfriends that adored her and girlfriends that respected her. In her high school years she became a true American, a member of the melting pot. She attributed much of her devotion to the Country from her 10th grade U.S. history class. Her teacher was a former Soviet diplomatic aide that emigrated 35 years earlier during the height of the Cold War. He worked in a farm machine factory for his first 20 years in the U.S. where he perfected his American English, became a citizen, raised a family, and made it his life's mission to spread the gospel of liberty and individual freedom in America. He went to college in the U.S. to become a high school history teacher. He taught her to love her country and showed her and his other students how horrible life could be elsewhere because of oppression, tyranny, or economic disincentives. Namia studied journalism and political science at the University of Virginia and landed the job as a reporter for ECF News, the most popular cable news channel.

The text message was from her college pal. It said that there was a terrorist on board an airplane that evening that had stabbed another passenger. She raced to the airport in her car and she called the airline's press office. She was going to break this news story. She knew that the best reporting depended on two things – accuracy and being first. She fostered the latter by having a wide network of friends and associates in news-generating places to notify her first. She nurtured these relationships by sharing credit, by sending gifts, or sending personal letters of thanks for the tips. She paid back with tickets to important events, too, whenever she could. She kept an extensive database of her contacts and what was important to them. For example, this college pal was a fan of football so she would remember to take her to a Redskins game next time she got a pair of tickets.

The airline would not say anything. She escalated her query with her charm. People knew the name Namia Pruvati if they watched ECF. She presented herself as polite, competent, and accurate. So when the airline's public relations officer was ready to release the story, she had a good chance of being first. That was the second aspect of being a great reporter – taking the time to be accurate. The people remembered whether you quoted them accurately. Whether the facts were correct. Whether other sources were included to ensure the best accuracy. She did her homework. She made sure that if there were two different opinions, she cited them that way. Then neither side made claims of inaccuracy. She remembered this from middle school, when the rumors about her and her friends were flying and were totally bogus. She swore then she would never spread rumors herself.

She arrived at the airport and started asking every curbside skycap about the incident, the ticket agents, and finally, she was pointed to a distressed looking individual sitting on a bench by the big windows. It was the ticket agent that sold the ticket to the man that was accused of doing the stabbing. Her perseverance paid off again. She interviewed the woman and learned that the passenger had a U.S. passport but he had a strong accent. The ticket agent had questioned the passenger because she knew something wasn't right. But there were no procedures she could invoke to deny him his ticket. She sold him the one-way ticket even though her gut told her not to.

Namia called her producer to tell him the story. He told her to line up her camera with her in front of the security line and then get the ticket agent on camera admitting she didn't want to sell the ticket to this passenger. Get whatever you can on film and we'll run you as soon as you're ready.

Namia smiled. She could do this. And she did.

* * * * *

The wall of televisions was flashing various headlines. Kale was jogging on his treadmill in his gym, which was adjacent to his office. He changed the speakers to the ECF News channel where Namia was about to report.

He thought back to the date he took her on a few years back, when she was just getting started in her career. He thought of the time he took her to Capitol Lounge and she was wide-eyed at the many famous people. He regretted, though, that he was unable to entice her loyalty with access to important people. She took the high road and would not compromise her journalistic integrity for his connections. She seemed to know his intentions before they sat down at the restaurant that evening. She announced to him first that she loved objective journalism more than fame and second she was committed to the truth, even if it meant she'd die of starvation. She then explained her parents' move to America and all that freedom had meant to them. And that freedom required exposing the truth about the actions people take, especially those people who have power. He had smiled politely and just quietly enjoyed the rest of the evening. He made no attempt to call her for another date after that.

Now as he watched her expose the ticket agent's story and the story of the passenger being stabbed, he realized her idealism and her pursuit of the truth served his goals much better than if he were controlling her access to news stories and what she would see in them. He smiled that the People would be clamoring for answers and angry about safety and demand more safety measures. He would gain more power as a result and soon he would have enough power to fix all the wrongs in the world. Just a little more time and Kale Evans would be the most powerful man in the world.

Crack, swoosh and … clunk. The billiard ball was struck solidly, rolled smoothly across the table, and plunked loudly into the corner pocket. A big smile crossed the lips of

President Percival Watsom Orinthbey. Secretary of State Bella Gliad congratulated the President on beating her again at billiards. "You are a master of the game, Perc," she breathed. She walked up to him and hugged him and he leaned down to kiss her. "But Bella, you make the game worth mastering." She blushed.

A tap at the door. "Come" announced POTUS.

An aide carefully opened the door, slid inside, shut the door behind him, walked over to the President, and handed him a small slip of paper. He stood silently waiting. The President looked at him and waved him out. The aide glided to the door, opened it carefully and slid outside, closing it again. Orinthbey grabbed the TV remote and turned the TV on. Bella asked, "What's wrong?" Orinthbey motioned for her to join him on the sofa. He clicked the rewind button until he saw the beginning of the clip with Namia Pruvati of ECF News telling the story of what happened at Reagan National airport. He jumped up and sent Bella out of the living room of the Camp David retreat, ordering her to get to work to quiet this story. He didn't want panic and he didn't want a big news story energizing his opponents. He called his aides in to begin damage control.

An hour later 300 phone calls and alerts had been sent out to directors across the government telling them to deflect from the man being a terrorist and to report that air travel was safe and that the government officials had everything under control and an investigation was underway.

Their official actions were everywhere within 20 minutes. Orinthbey watched as his media helpers drowned out the voice of Namia and her ticket agent. Later Bella came in to tell Percival that the FBI had arrived at the hospital to speak with the passenger that claimed she was stabbed. The news was already being released that she was a disturbed woman, prone to making up stories for attention, and that she inflicted the cut on herself after the turbulence just to get her husband's attention. By the 10pm news experts were being interviewed on the strange behaviors people engage in when stressed or when needing attention.

The Brain called. "P.W.?"

"Yes, Mr. Star, how are you this evening?"

"You need to decide whether you are serving your country at my bequest or for your own interest."

"I don't understand? I would think you would want the mistakes of the TSA tempered."

"Mistakes! No, actually, I think the angle is the TSA didn't do enough. We need to get the people into a frenzy that we need more prevention when traveling to prevent mentally unstable people from boarding."

"Yes, Mr. Star."

"And besides, this woman was promoting *the Bill of Rights*!" Star shouted this into Percival's ear.

Perc weighed his remark. "Really? I thought she was a mother-of-four."

"Look, Miss-terr President," Star aspirated. "My guy, a psychiatrist, discovered she attended a march on the Capitol this morning. He also found her to be an attention-seeking neglected and deranged housewife. We can't control the People if they're spouting old-fashioned individual rights." Their goal was to expand government's ability to search and control the citizens. "The angle is simple. Neither the student nor the mother should be traveling unless the TSA decides they are fit to do so. The safety and convenience of all passengers must be assured."

"Yes, of course." Orinthbey tried to regain the upper-hand in the conversation.

"Next I want you to schedule time with Congressman Blake. He has proposed legislation drafted by one our staffers that will allow the TSA to access medical records to see if citizens have any mental issues before they're allowed to fly. That would have prevented this crazy woman from making this scene in the first place and saved the rest of the passengers the inconvenience of flying to the wrong city. And I think it also includes a provision that when a person flies, they have to disclose the purpose of their trip before they're allowed through the security checkpoint. I think Blake's people have drafted a form to use for that purpose, too."

"Yes, Mr. Star."

"Oh and one more thing, make a speech in the next day or two to console the travelers that were inconvenienced, and announce the new plans. But meet with Blake first. I think that should do it."

"Yes, Mr. Star."

"And so you're in the loop, we have some people lined up to voice their complaints about being inconvenienced because the flight landed in Atlanta, rather than Jacksonville. They will also speak to how crazy she was before this happened."

Orinthbey looked at the phone when he hung up. Yes, he wanted more power; yes he wanted to solve the world's problems. Star's plan sounded like a good one – make travel safer by knowing more about the bad guys and their plans. But right now he didn't feel much drive to do this or Star's other plans. Star meddled too much and too often. Perc was President, after all, not Star. Perc wanted to keep everything the way it is. His wife left him after the election, lifting a huge weight from his back and shoulders. She took all four of the whiney kids with her so he was a bachelor now. He discovered that he loved the power of the Presidency, with staff waiting on him all the time, the attention he received, the special treatment everywhere he went, all the important people who wanted his attention.

His best decision was when he had nominated the former CIA Director, Bella Gliad, to be his Secretary of State. She knew all about the world, its dangers, America's enemies, and the capabilities of the U.S. She knew everything to protect him and run the foreign affairs part of the Presidency. She was really good at her job. So he could play, party, and be a figure-head. She was so charmed that he nominated her that she sent him a gift – a glass-framed, new condition baseball card of Hank Aaron from the 1963 season. As he studied the gift, he remembered his childhood, the excitement of baseball games all season, trading cards with his friends, playing ball himself. Baseball was his passion. Boyish jubilation is what he felt gazing at this gift. He called Bella to the White House to have lunch with him the day after the inauguration parties and they chatted for hours. He realized that she was once a beauty – a type of intelligent-looking beauty – though the years had made an effect. But she was still desirable. He gave her a tour of the White House after lunch and she seemed to know about every painting and the major events that took place in every room. He knew then he had to see her again.

He called her the next day and asked her to brief him on her travel plans for the coming quarter. She came to the White House again and briefed the entire team about her travel plans. His new cabinet and his transition team advisors were impressed with her knowledge of the hotspots around the world and how to address them. She then looked Percival straight in the eye and boldly suggested he accompany her to three of the cities on her travel plan list. She followed that by explaining what the benefits and risks were to visiting those locations. He looked around the room and asked the others if there were any reasons they could object to her plans at State and there were none. He looked back at her and studied her face for a moment and announced, "I like how you present your Department, Madame Secretary. I would be honored to accompany you on the trip this quarter." She gave him a knowing look and he felt himself getting warmer, redder, and he realized he felt like a teenager again. He popped out of his chair and left the room.

Since then they became close companions and he was happy about that, too. A few of his closest staff might know they spent a lot of time together, but otherwise, there were no rumors or suggestions about their private life.

Percival Orinthbey didn't really see why Mr. Star was so intent on making a big deal about this airplane incident and the overblown reporting by ECF News. He decided that because he was President, Mr. Star could no longer push him around. He called out to Rebecca, his assistant, to tell his press secretary to make a statement to the news media that ECF should get its facts straight before making an irresponsible report that could cause people to lose faith in their government and its systems. Next he had Rebecca make sure that Congressman Blake could meet him at the White House Monday morning sometime. Last he told her to schedule a 15 minute speech from the oval office Monday night.

Rebecca called back, "Monday night football is on Monday night. What time do you want to be on?"

"You decide. Don't piss off too many Americans!"

FOUR

Saturday Night, Atlanta Hartsfield Airport

The plane landed. Jake was swept outside and down a staircase onto the tarmac by the airline's representative. He stood at the bottom of the stairs dazed while a black SUV drove up in front of him. He was pulled to the car door and he climbed in. There was a man sitting in the backseat with him.

"Jake, my name is Dr. Hildebrand. I'm a psychiatrist hired by the airline to explain what happened. Has your wife been making comments about conspiracies and far out notions about the government? This is a common problem for women in their 30s, especially women who have so many children to take care of and the responsibilities of her job. Her stress levels surely must be high. It's a common affliction for women to go through such a 'mid-life' crisis. They do this to get attention. They want their husbands to have to drop everything and pay attention only to them. Which is exactly what you're doing. You had to drop everything today to be here. My colleagues did a psychiatric evaluation of her this evening and we found she has delusions of grandeur, big notions of a conspiracy that only she can solve, and then she becomes a victim and must be rescued by her Prince Charming – you."

"What are you talking about?" Jake asked in a dazed and confused manner.

"I'm just letting you know her injury was minor. A man with a plastic knife, which was served with his food on the airplane, was returning from the rest room with it in his hand. The man was being transferred from one institution for mentally deficient people to another and was carrying the plastic knife like a microphone as he sang songs. Then the plane hit some turbulence and he bumped into your wife while she was heading to the rest room. That's all. She wanted you to come here to pay attention to her."

Jake was shaking his head. What was real? What was the truth? Who was this guy? "Let me see your I.D." he finally mustered.

"Sure!" Dr. Hildebrand brandished his glossy, full color photo I.D. from the Johns Hopkins School of Medicine showing he was not only a psychiatrist there but also a Fellow in the American Psychiatric Association.

The car arrived and Jake walked shakily with the airline representative by one arm and Dr. Hildebrand by the other arm. They went through the double sliding glass doors to the elevator and waited. Jake was still contemplating what he had heard. The airline didn't say these things. The airline made it sound like she was attacked. But of course the airline doesn't want it to appear that a terrorist boarded their airplane.

He walked into her hospital room. Though he had planned to be strong and supportive of Mari to reassure her that she did the right thing joining the *Bill of Rights Restoration* march, he was overcome by what he saw. She was in intensive care, with respirators, stomach pumps, air tubes, and machines glowing. She was asleep and didn't see him. He walked over and took her hand into his and sobbed, putting his face in her hand. The two men left the room while Jake sobbed. Even they couldn't stand by to watch a grown man so affected.

The street was dark. The house was dark. Jazz pulled into the driveway, grabbed her iPad and iPhone out of their chargers and shoved them into her bag. She climbed out of the Honda Pilot, walked around back and pulled her duffle bag out. She pressed the button to lock the doors of her vehicle and walked to the front door. She rang the doorbell. The neighbor peaked through the curtain, turned on the front porch light, peaked through the curtain again, unlocked the door, and opened it. But rather than letting Jazz in, she stepped out onto the porch. She let Jazz know the kids were all in bed and kept asking where their Dad was. Then she abruptly left. Jazz called after her, "Thanks Mrs. Pitt. My parents will be here tomorrow so we won't need your help again." But she was already out of earshot.

Jazz turned on the TV to watch the news. She quickly became infuriated at the suggestions that her sister was deranged, needed attention, and made up a story so she would have to go to the hospital. Jazz muted the TV, went into the kitchen and grabbed a beer from the refrigerator, poured some potato chips into a bowl, and returned to the sofa. She pulled out her iPad and checked *The Drudge Report* first.

Matt Drudge became famous for being first and covering the gambit of politics, weather, and gossip. David McClintick called him a modern-day Tom Paine. A popular, well read town crier with 3,000,000 unique visitors each month.

There it was. In the third column, about one-third down on the page were two links. The first said "Mother of four hysterical on flight to Florida". Below that was another link "Ticket agent for Reliable Airlines didn't want to sell ticket to passenger". Jazz smiled. Drudge was an expert at picking stories, laying out his web page of headlines, and titling stories to make them seem more enticing than they were.

She clicked the first story. "AFP reports that a 32-year-old mother of four, needing attention from her busy husband, concocted a story about being stabbed on a flight from Virginia to Jacksonville. In reality there was turbulence on the plane that caused her and another passenger, both standing in the aisle, though the seat belt sign was illuminated, to bump into each other. The other passenger was holding his plastic utensils from dinner, apparently to put them in the trash receptacle at the back of the plane. The woman complained of stomach pains and then made an overblown effort to faint in the aisle, leaving the pilot no choice but to land at the nearest airport. Reliable Airlines has already sent both passengers to the local hospital for evaluation. The remaining passengers were boarded on busses for the remaining 350 miles to Jacksonville."

'Wow. Talk about spin.' Jasmine thought.

She clicked on the second story. It was a link to a video, rather than a written report. It was the clip of Namia Pruvati speaking with the ticket agent at Reagan National. Jasmine clicked the link at the top of the page next to Namia's name. It opened her email client with the email address that would arrive in Namia's email box eventually. She wrote, "This is Jasmine Roberts. I'm the sister of the passenger that was stabbed. I just watched your report. Please call me." Jasmine typed in her cell phone number and her email address and clicked "send".

She shook her head to herself. She knew Mari was sane. She knew Mari well enough to know she wasn't doing anything to get attention from Jake. She knew what Jake had gone through after hearing from the airline himself. So she sat and pondered that Mari's urgings for Jasmine to get involved and to pay attention are not only sincere but well-founded. Jazz was so busy selling electronics, making money, playing hard, and enjoying life, she hadn't wanted to believe Mari's pleadings that bad people had taken over most positions of power throughout the government and were now using that power to pursue their own ends, rather than protecting the rights of citizens as the Founders fought for. And to discredit her sister in an effort to cover-up a terrorist attack on a commercial jet.

She returned to the fridge and pulled out the ingredients to make a sandwich. She put one together and grabbed another beer. Then she walked over to the bookcase in the family room of Mari and Jake's house and pulled down some of the books Mari had been asking her to read the past couple of years. She started with <u>The 5000 Year Leap</u> by W. Cleon Skousen. 'Might as well read them alphabetically.' she thought.

The girl didn't even look 18 yet. Under her black hat and black eye shadow, she was youthful and should have been hopeful for a promising future. Instead she was with a guy who looked like a dirt bag. He was wearing a black leather jacket with satanic symbols. J.B. shook his head in disgust. Riding the train home was no longer amusing. He once would look at such people as merely trying to be different, trying to rebel in order to grow up. Now he looked at them as emblematic of the decline in America. These young people enjoy being free to wear such trash but at the same time have no idea *why* they are free to do so.

J.B. pulled out his iPad and checked the Drudge Report's headlines. There were the stories of the attack on the airplane. After watching Namia's report, he called her. She didn't answer so he left her a message.

"Namia, it's me, J.B. Please let me know what else you learn on this news story about the airplane. Thanks."

J.B. served on the Transportation Committee so he felt personally responsible if the Nation's transportation system wasn't working, as it should, apparent from one passenger being stabbed by another!

* * * * *

"Yes, Mr. Star." Kale answered the phone. He didn't want to speak with the Brain just now. He was working on devising his plans and needed to concentrate.

"Kale. Get down there to ECF News and pull some strings to stop their continuing investigation of this crazy woman on the airplane. Use whatever resources you need to." That meant bribes.

"Mr. Star, need I remind you I have tried to reach Ms. Pruvati before. She cannot be purchased. She has no price."

The Brain harrumphed. Everyone had a price. "Try negative rewards rather than positive ones." Kale didn't like the sound of "negative" rewards. That wasn't his territory. Mr. Star had other people that he called for knee-breaking and other persuasive measures. He replied that he would try his charm again but for more persuasive means, the Brain would have to hire "Bo", the rehabilitated petty-crimes perpetrator that did Star's dirty work. "Mr. Star, I will call on Ms. Pruvati and her producer. I will remind them of their responsibility to provide objective reporting and not to cause unnecessary panic and to be supportive of the efforts of the agencies and personnel who keep us safe each day. But I suggest you call Bo if you want her tires slashed or her house vandalized."

Star shouted into the phone, "Don't speak to me about tire slashing and vandalism. You know I don't participate in that stuff!" The words were sprayed into the phone with disgust. Kale laughed to himself as he pressed the "Stop Record" button on his phone. He hung up. He knew that even though he made Star yell and shout, he was also Star's best organizer. He had delivered dozens of organizers of top caliber to Star. These guys controlled tens of thousands of people dedicated to their causes, unions and special interest groups, people with an agenda that wasn't being met in the current system. This army would be ready when Star pulled the lever. Or, when Kale pulled the lever for Star. They all needed Star's money but Kale still controlled the communications. Even though Star was dedicated to the cause and had made many nudges in the right direction, he hadn't started the changeover yet. For months he told Kale the time hadn't come yet. Kale admired the steps taken, however small, in setting up an elaborate scheme to take power. But these trickles weren't tidal waves. And though Kale was okay with the trickles of new power most of the time because he could see their effects, he was now ready for a wave, a big wave. They were so close to taking power, one single tidal wave would be enough energy to finish the job to end capitalism and greed and replace it with a fairer system, where everyone would be fed, housed, safe, and get along. And Kale knew he would oversee the whole thing. He already had the organizers in place. They were ready to take over enough local police departments, fire departments, schools, hospitals, transportation means, and the food supply. He didn't have the communications piece in place yet to control all the news, especially among individuals. But he had a solution to that piece. Yes, he was ready *now*. At age 54, the time for *him* was now. He wanted to have some years to enjoy the new world.

Kale stopped his daydreaming. First he called his assistant, Ritalia, to come help him with this assignment. Then he clicked the keys on his workstation keyboard to research this Mari, her family, her neighbors, everything he could get. He learned about a sister, her age, where she worked, where she lived, whether she paid her bills, and so on. And he studied the neighbors. And the friends in this circle that babysat for each other. One couple included a Muslim husband and a Christian wife. That would be the angle he would work. Then he called his hacker-on-staff, Ralphie, and asked him to see if he could sabotage ECF's footage.

* * * * *

After the calls were made, the FBI was in place, the broadcast news channels were on message, Percival felt he could relax. He dialed Bella. She would be in the front conference room running her angle of the message as he worked in his office. She answered, "Yes, Mr. President?"

"Bella, I'm done making calls at my end. It looks like the damage control efforts are working fine. I'm going to retire now to my quarters. However, I would like to hear your report from State tonight, rather than in the morning, as soon as you are ready. Is that understood?" He added a sharpness to the question to assert his presidential prerogative.

Bella took several moments before she intimated, "I will give you a report from State as soon as I can this evening, delivered to your quarters, as you request, Mr. President." Then she breathed a suggestive sigh. "Will that meet your demands, sir?" she added.

"Yes. Very good." he added in his stern voice. But he smiled ear-to-ear. Yes, he enjoyed life very much these days. Bella was perfect. He would enjoy her company tonight. He was the President. And he was on top of the world.

Late that night, as Jake slept at Mari's bedside, he felt her hand twitch inside of his. He roused himself awake and looked up at her. Her eyes were blinking. She was waking up. He felt an enormous relief. Her hand was warm and she had a glow about her, despite her ordeal. He stood up over her and smiled, his tears now gone. He said "Hi, Sleepy". Her lips curved slightly and she whispered back, "Hi". Jake was overcome with joy that Mari was okay. Then her face grew serious and she drew up her strength and quietly asked, "Did they get him?" Jake felt awful. No one told him what happened to the bad guy and he hadn't watched the news nor asked anyone. To be honest he would say he didn't know. But he wanted her to use all her strength to heal and not to worry.

He said, "Yes, they got him. He was contained on an airplane, remember?"

Mari fell back asleep. And Jake stepped into the hall to call Jasmine to ask her what the news was.

FIVE

Sunday, Mari's house in Florida

Jasmine awoke with a start. As she blinked her eyes, her niece climbed onto the couch to join her and snuggle up. Jasmine quickly became conscious and realized she was on her sister's sofa and it was morning. What a pleasant surprise in the morning to have her niece join her. She lay still and awake deciding she would make her famous pancakes for breakfast for the children.

As she rolled off the sofa, she looked at her phone and saw there was a voice message. She refreshed in the bathroom, checked her message and heard that Namia Pruvati had called her back in the middle of the night. The message was "Hello Jasmine. This is Namia Pruvati of ECF News. Yes, I would like to speak with you about your sister. Call me back at this number at your convenience. I checked with my producer and if you are interested we can fly you to Virginia to interview you in our studio Sunday afternoon and again Monday. We will cover your expenses."

Jasmine jumped into the shower and thought about this proposition. She had decided last night upon hearing the news of her sister that it was time for her to get involved, not that anyone could have prevented a crazy person from stabbing her sister. But it was because her sister was trying to solve these problems that she got stabbed. And she thought what better way to make a statement on behalf of the country than on National TV.

As she dried off she called her parents in Ohio. No answer. They must be on their way to Florida. As she pulled on her clothes she tried to call Jake to ask how Mari was doing. He didn't answer his phone. So she left a message asking about Mari and about him. She called her boss. He answered the phone and told her to take as much time as he needed. (He had heard the news about the stabbing but didn't know that was Jasmine's older sister.) Done in the bathroom, Jazz went to the kitchen and started brewing the coffee and heating the griddle. She saved the call to ECF News for last. As she dialed, the kids came out to see her wiping their sleepy eyes. They asked about Mom and Dad. Jasmine explained that their Mom's plane had to stop half way home because Mom needed to see a doctor and Dad went to be with Mom. So that's why Aunt Jazz was here. They were fine with that. Jazz poured her coffee and went to the griddle where she poured batter onto the pan. The kids squealed with delight at the prospect of pancakes. Aunt Jazz always made pancakes when she was visiting in the mornings.

After breakfast, the children went to their playroom to play and Jazz pulled out her phone. It was already 9:30. She dialed the number and on the first ring the familiar-sounding voice of Namia Pruvati answered.

"Namia Pruvati here."

"Hi Namia. This is Jasmine Roberts. I got your message this morning. And I'm returning your call."

"Hi Ms. Roberts. I'm so sorry about your sister. Have you spoken with her yet?" Always looking for more to the story.

"Please call me Jazz. No. I tried to call my brother-in-law this morning but his phone just rings and rings and rolls over to voice mail. I'm here with their kids."

"That's so good of you to take care of their kids. How many do they have?"

"There are 4 delightful children."

"I'm sure they are. What are their names?"

"I'd rather not say. Mari likes to keep her family life private."

"I understand. Are they boys, girls, or what mix?"

Jasmine laughed. As a salesperson, she knew the value of getting as much information as possible from her clients, whether it seemed relevant or not, it could be of use later. And of course, reporters want to paint a picture, as complete as possible, and are looking for the facts to fill in the missing parts of that picture. "Mari has 2 girls and 2 boys, the oldest is 8 and the youngest is 2."

Namia knew that laugh – it was a *knowing* laugh. "Thank you for sharing what you can. I'm sure Mari is a wonderful mother and I know this is a tragic event to have occurred to a typical, church-going mom. The Nation needs to know such crimes are being committed and pour their outrage into appropriate measures of self-defense and asking their representatives to enact meaningful policies in light of the facts of this crime."

Jasmine paused. She let that sink in. "Yes, your job is an important one, essential to a well-functioning republic. And yes, your account is accurate." She paused. "So what is the deal with the guy that stabbed my sister?"

"He is a Yemeni citizen. He just arrived in the U.S. yesterday to attend a small college in Jacksonville. He had a plastic knife and that knife stabbed your sister in the abdomen. It isn't completely clear whether it was an accident from turbulence, or a deliberate assault. He's being held by the FBI as we speak and they won't say anything else. My colleague at ECF is handling that part of the story." Namia concluded the call. "Look, grab any flight you can today to Reagan National Airport. Call my producer, Gary Wise, as soon as your plane lands and he'll send a car to pick you up and take you to the studio. We'll have a make-up person help you. Wear what you want to wear on TV when you arrive at the studio. Solids are better than noisy prints. We'll put you up at the Green Garden hotel in Crystal City tonight and have you back to the studio again on Monday. Thanks for taking the time to help the Press fulfill its obligation to report the news and keep a check on the government."

"See you later today." Jasmine replied weakly.

She cleaned up the breakfast dishes, checked on the kids, packed up her things, and checked her iPad for flights. There were flights leaving at noon, 1pm, 3pm, and 5pm. She needed to know when her parents were arriving. She tried to call them again. She wished they would invest in a cell phone.

Just then the house phone rang and it was her parents saying their flight just landed, they were heading to the car rental counter, and would be at Mari's house in an hour. Jazz gave them an update about Mari, about her plans to go to ECF Studios, and asked them to reach Jake since the two of them kept missing each other.

Jasmine was about to choose the 1pm flight but she looked at the clothes she had packed in her overnight bag. Ugh. She decided she would stop at the shopping mall on the way to the airport and buy a new suit. She booked the 3pm flight instead.

His thoughts returned to work as soon as he heard the phone ring. It had been late when he got home last night. He looked at the display.

"Good morning Namia. What's new?" J.B. didn't mind his weekend being interrupted for cause, in this case transportation matters and matters of importance to the

Nation, which was his purpose in being a Representative in the first place.

"Hey J.B. I spoke with the sister of the mom who was attacked on the plane. She's on her way to the studio and should be here this evening. I'll be interviewing her to do a story on the victim, how the victim is a typical American, that sort of thing. I haven't learned any more yet from the airline or NTSB. Both seem to be buttoned down. The FBI is holding a Yemeni national that arrived in the U.S. yesterday to attend college in Jacksonville. Not certain whether it was deliberate or accidental. Monty is handling that angle."

"Do you need me for the piece today, or just tomorrow?"

"Actually, we could link you up from home this evening and have you in the studio tomorrow. But if you can come in live tonight and appear live on the morning show tomorrow that would be even better."

He did not hesitate. "I'll be at the studio in time for 6 tonight, okay?"

"Great. Thanks J.B." and Namia hung up. She then went back to calling her contacts at the FAA, NTSB and the airline. Her producer called her and said he was trying to reach the family at the hospital, and the lawyer for the assailant. He had all the specifics on the arrest and a statement from the arresting officer.

Jasmine was feeling euphoric. She had come to know that when she was on a new adventure, her endorphins were released and that was why she played hard, worked hard, and loved life so much. She had purchased a royal blue business suit and matching shoes. She wore a high collar shirt that was soft looking but crisp. A new suit, a new adventure, and a new opportunity and she felt on top of the world.

She headed for the security checkpoint at the gate. The agent pulled her aside to go through the full-body scanner. She refused. The agent behind her shouted "OPT OUT" making her cringe. The next agent had her stand in a glass box to wait until a pat-down could be done. Jazz looked at her watch. She felt her throat constricting and ache. She felt her heart start pounding and her blood vessels dilate as the extra blood volume moved to her extremities in the fight or flight response. Her palms became sweaty. And she felt pins and needles in the ball of both hands. Anger was rising inside her. She was not a terrorist. Wasn't it obvious? She was on a business trip. Can they not see that? Why on earth should she be put into a prison cell in the middle of plain view? She looked around her. She saw a man holding his camera up in front of his body and it was pointed in her direction. She wondered if she was being filmed by him. Then it occurred to her that if she were being filmed and that man later saw her on TV he would know it's her. She was feeling ashamed. Her temper was beyond a simmer and now at rolling boil. She surveyed the room around her again. She saw at least 8 sets of eyes on her. *Why won't anyone do something to stop this? Are they stunned silent? Or are they trained to accept it? Do they think it's okay because I'm not being physically harmed? Well what about the emotional harm I am undergoing?*, she thought.

Finally after 12 minutes standing in the box, a beefy woman in uniform came up to the door, unlocked it, and asked Jasmine to step out. She brought her to a two-sided space and with gloved hands started to move her hands down Jasmine's slim arms. The TSA agent explained she would next run her hands under Jasmine's breasts. Jasmine felt cold. She wanted to say *something* but she couldn't find her voice. She heard the agent raise her voice and she came back to the reality of her situation. The agent was asking her to raise her arms to her sides. Finally Jasmine mustered to say, "How can you live with yourself knowing you are searching innocent Americans without probable cause?" The agent moved her hands under and around Jasmine's breasts. She didn't answer. But she did say, "Next I'll be moving my hands down your front, between and down your legs. Then I'll have you turn around and I'll do the same on your backside." Jasmine now grew stronger and persisted. "I asked you a question. Is it that you are just 'doing your job'?" The agent responded as she pressed her hands firmly between Jasmine's legs under her skirt. Jasmine's face got hot with embarrassment. She had never been touched by a woman. She had never been touched like this. She wondered if this is what a woman went through at the beginning of a rape. The agent finally said "Turn around" ignoring Jasmine. Jazz kept it up, "Do you believe in the Constitution because, if you do, you are violating part of the Bill of Rights right now. How can you live with yourself?" The agent moved down Jasmine's back and shoved her hands up the back side of Jasmine's skirt, between her legs. Jasmine screamed "Get your hands out of my crotch!" The agent pressed a buzzer next to her. Within 30 seconds 5 more agents were surrounding Jasmine. Jasmine shouted with indignation "This … this…. agent shoved her hands up my crotch!" One male agent chuckled and said "Well you must not have been cooperatin'." Jazz looked around her. The man with the cell phone was still standing 30 feet away with his phone up and toward her. She deflected their concern and continued shouting "and I'm being filmed by that guy over there!" The laughing agent sprinted across the space and around the machines toward camera-phone man, who saw the agent coming and was already beyond their lines and into the crowds out of reach of the agent. She didn't stop the tirade, "Don't you people realize you are violating our rights?"

Two agents each grabbed an arm and forced her to walk to the wall and through a door into an enclosed "office" space of sorts, though there was no furniture, no windows, and a strange looking device on the door handle. She knew she was disheveled. Her muscles were aching, her head was hurting, and her skin was flushed, though she felt cold and was trying to fend off the shivers. A rotund man with red splotchy skin and a bald head came in. His back was to her as he pushed buttons on the door handle device. Jasmine didn't like this one bit. Her instincts reminded her she was vulnerable. A prisoner. This man was between her and the only door. The door was probably locked so she couldn't get out. The space was small but probably also sound-proofed. She could scream and no one would come to rescue her. This man could do anything and she would be helpless to stop him, get help, or escape. She knew then she had to rely on her wits to get out of this. She reached into her pocket and pressed the familiar button on her cell phone to begin filming the scene. The lens might not be able to see anything but it would surely record all the sounds. Then she moved against the left wall, freeing her strong side toward him and giving her leverage against the wall, if she needed it.

He began by looking at her ticket and her ID, which he had in his hand. "Ms. Roberts, if you still want to catch your airplane today, you will go through the scanner. Our agent tried to conduct a pat-down in lieu of the scanner but you made a scene. So you will have to submit to the scanner." He waited for a reply. Jasmine decided she would not say anything unless she was asked a reasonable question. She was certain she was being recorded by them and she knew that even though they violated her 4th amendment rights, she wouldn't willingly give up her 5th amendment rights as well. "Ms. Roberts, if you do not willingly submit to the scanner, we will arrest you for failing to comply with the TSA's air travel regulations. Jasmine did not hear a question. Why didn't he just ask her? At this point, there was no way she would submit to the scanner. The five agents back there and this guy would all save a copy for their personal use! Then when they found out she'd be on TV today and tomorrow, they would share it with others and perhaps use it to blackmail her later in life. Nope. No way. He continued, "Ms. Roberts, I just started my shift. I'm here all day. You, on the other hand, will miss your flight if you do not get through our security checkpoint." Was that a threat she wondered? He would think of it as a fact. But she saw it as an abuse of power. She thought back to a novel Mari had her read called *Patriots*. In that story the entire country fell into anarchy after inflation spiraled out of control. In the aftermath gangs would roadblock roads and force people who wanted to pass down the roads with heavy "taxes" or "tolls" to pass. If they didn't willingly comply, they would be shot and robbed anyway. The gang members came to see themselves as reasonable. They maintained the road and they charged a tax for people to use the road, just like governments had done before they collapsed. The gangs convinced themselves they were doing an honorable service so long as people willingly complied. And they convinced themselves they were being fair to all by punishing those that failed to comply with their "law". She considered *what if* government gets in the hands of the robbers, burglars, and looters? That's when we have tyranny. And she thought this felt like tyranny. She hadn't done anything wrong and she was being treated like a criminal for not willingly complying with this gang. She wondered if she should ask her questions of this guy. She thought not, she was boxed in and wasn't going to be let out. She felt like sitting. But she decided she would not show any sign of giving up. She was also tempted to look at her watch to see whether she had missed her plane or not. No, if she did that, it would be a sign to him that she was impatient and willing to submit. She decided she would sit here all night if she had to. Missing her plane just gave her more to tell Namia in her interview with ECF News later. That would help her in her new mission: to do everything she could to fix this for *every honest American*.

Several minutes had passed. Then the rotund TSA manager turned his back to unlock the door. She wondered if she should rush out behind him or not. He hadn't said whether she should have to wait or not. She figured she would be shot before she could get far if she rushed. She felt relieved so far. But she shouldn't let her guard down. As he opened the door, he turned to her and told her to wait. He closed the door and was gone.

She sighed. Her bodily functions seemed to have returned to normal. Was she getting used to this treatment?

She weighed the possibilities. She might be allowed to proceed to her plane – 20% chance of that. She might be arrested – 10% chance of that. She might have to sit in this room for hours, miss her flight, while they tried to pressure her into being scanned – 60% chance of that. And maybe a 10% chance that they would redo the pat-down. She decided then she could live with any of those possibilities. Except maybe the pat-down. But this time, she had a video recording going and she would protest loudly during a pat-down. She would say they already had groped her crotch, and she'd make a fuss. If they arrested her she would start her line of questioning again about her 4th amendment rights. Then she wondered if she was missing any possibilities.

She looked at her watch. She had 25 minutes until the plane left. She decided she would never make it. Jasmine spent the time remembering every detail of her ordeal so she could tell Namia later. But she did it inside her head, not out loud, believing she was probably being surveilled in this room. She figured she and the manager were in here several minutes and altogether she had been in security about 90 minutes so far. She peaked at her camera in her pocket. It was still running and filming. She had plenty of disk space, too.

She heard the door lock clicking. She dropped her camera into her pocket. A female agent walked in. This woman had a crew cut, no makeup, a bulldog face, thick legs, and a tire of fat around her waist. She also had huge breasts that rested on top of her tire. She began, "Ms. Roberts, we have elected to allow you to proceed through this security checkpoint if you will submit to a strip search. You will have to remove your suit and shirt, strip to your bra and panties and allow me to do a pat down. Do you agree to a strip search?" Crap, thought Jasmine, this was a possibility she hadn't imagined. Such is life. She decided this would be a juicier story to tell on National TV tonight but she also figured they had cameras running in here. Jasmine replied, "Do you have cameras in this room? Do you have x-rays through its walls? Will images of my body be taken anyway as I am searched in this room?" The agent didn't respond. But she looked up toward the ceiling. Jasmine said, "I see that you do. I won't agree to a strip search. I'm an American citizen. I'm not suspected of a crime and therefore you cannot search me. I just won't fly today if you refuse to let me through the check point. And I'll expect the TSA to refund my ticket price if I miss my flight." The agent harrumphed and turned to leave.

Jasmine thought about all this. She would be imaged in the x-ray machine or she would be imaged-in this room. What about the people doing the pat-downs? Do they get imaged, too, without realizing it? She thought it's possible that in the gloves of the agents, they might be measuring something about the travelers. What on earth could the government want with images of all American citizens? Is it some sort of national identification?

She looked at her watch again. She knew now they were watching her. She knew they knew she was about to miss her flight. She figured it was on purpose. They were wielding their power. They may not even be thinking to themselves, "Let's show her our power". But they know how much time she has. They know they have the power to let her through or not. They didn't like her outburst and they are letting her know they can make her stop next time.

Three minutes before her flight's scheduled departure, the manager agent returned to the room, held the door open for her, and told her they had checked out her passport while she was waiting and they decided she was not a risk and she could pass. She didn't respond. She walked with him to the exit of the security area and headed for the gate. She pulled out her cell phone, texted her airline with her ticket number, and hoped they would wait for her. As she trotted to her gate, the ticket agent smiled at her and said "You just made it; the captain had 2 procedures he had to add before we could close the doors!" Jasmine called back over her shoulder as she trotted down the jetway, "Those TSA people are going to be the death of your airline!"

SIX

Sunday Evening, ECF Studio, Crystal City, Virginia

In a large, overstuffed leather recliner, Jasmine felt her body sink into the comfort of the chair as she relaxed. It had been a horrible time at the airport but the flight was smooth, her transport from the airport to the studio was uneventful, and she was left alone for a few minutes while the make-up specialist stepped out for a moment, before doing her face for an interview on ECF news. The producer was incredibly handsome and she felt safe in his presence. He was cordial and attentive as he greeted her and explained the entire process of being interviewed for the news. After the explanation, she told him about her ordeal. She told him she recorded much of her ordeal and that someone was there filming her. She handed her phone to this *Adonis* so he could upload her recording. He came into the make-up room to tell her that her footage was fantastic and they would like to use it. He handed her a form to sign to waive any legal rights to contest its use on ECF News or whomever ECF decides to share it with. Then he sat down with her and showed her some footage of herself at the airport on his iPad. She recognized herself standing in the booth at the airport. The Adonis producer was elated when she confirmed that the footage was of her. He explained that the filmmaker is a local freelancer that reports on transportation for ECF. He takes footage at airports all over Florida and sends them to ECF. Just then he touched the top of her hand and thanked her for stepping up, making the trip, and helping ECF. He gave her a winning smile and apologized that he had to leave her now, because he had to assemble the footage into a news story that would fit in the time slot they had. Jasmine glowed in a comfortable serenity that his presence had given her. Her hand was still warm from his touch. She couldn't remember his name but he seemed like an angel.

The make-up technician came in and spent about 15 minutes putting thick gobs of brownish goo on her face. Her caked face felt heavy enough to crack and come off in chunks. She smiled slightly to see whether it would cleave, but saw her reflection transform her from a fresh-faced outdoorsy girl into a glamorous model. She thought of Narcissus for a moment as she realized she could get used to the cake on her face.

The door glided open and J.B. strolled in to the makeup room. He walked straight over to her and confidently introduced himself, "Ms. Roberts? My name is J.B. Stanton. I'm a member of the Transportation committee in the U.S. House of Representatives. I will be discussing your sister's incident on tonight's news in the same segment that you will be on. I want to wish you the best of luck. And please let me know if you have any questions about how they do things here. I'm on often and know the ropes." Jasmine was rarely at a loss for words. As a salesperson she was a great listener but also knew how to talk, how to make others feel engaged, how to take control of a situation, and how not to feel intimidated by the CEOs and executives at big corporations that she sold her wares to. But when this Congressman walked in, his charisma and persona took up the whole room and she was unable to find any words to respond. She stammered out, "Hi. Uh - nice to meet you." He sized her up just then. She felt his piercing gaze take in her face, hair, and body. She felt more exposed now than she did during the TSA search. He said, "You are a very brave citizen to stand before millions of Americans to share the truth about your sister. More Americans should be as responsible as you. I'll be going on in a moment. You can watch right here." He pointed to a TV behind her. She looked up as he walked past her to turn on the TV set, reaching up above her. She caught his scent and felt dizzy, attributing it to the whirlwind 24 hours she had been through already. As he stood above her, she looked up at him and felt a buzz in the air between them, like an electric spark across the space. She regained control of herself and suddenly stood up from her big chair to introduce herself more commandingly. But, she clumsily misjudged the distance between them, of which there was not enough to leave a space. She pushed her right hand forward to offer a handshake but his body was so close that her hand pushed into his chest. He looked down at her hand and rather than shake back, he took her hand into both of his, looked at it for a moment, then looked back at her and told her, "You will do great on TV, I just know it." He slipped past her and moved silently to the door and was gone. Jasmine sat back down wondering what just transpired. It was magical; he was magical. High energy surrounds him. She thought about what he had said and she realized not only did she appreciate his confidence, but also knew that she would do fine on TV. She looked up at the set and saw Namia being interviewed by the anchor. She was explaining all the facts so far. Then the anchor introduced and began asking questions of Congressman Stanton. Congressman? She thought he looked too young and seemed too sincere to be a congressman.

Just then, the producer, whom she had earlier dubbed Adonis, came in to get her. He brought her to a tiny studio room that had a fancy poster with a scene of the airport set behind a small desk. Adonis asked her to sit at the desk and look up. In front of her was a large lens with a light beneath it. Above the lens was a display. There she could see the anchor asking questions of someone else. She was told he would ask her questions and she should respond briefly and concisely. Adonis recommended pausing slightly to speak rather than starting with an "um". He told her they would do a dry run to see how she looks and sounds on camera and that she would not yet be on the air. The light next to the lens would be red, however, to indicate the camera lens was on, so they could monitor what she said and how she looked during this test interview. (It also meant they were recording but he didn't tell her that.) He suggested she should sit on her hands to avoid touching her face during the interview and to avoid talking with her hands, which can be distracting to the viewers. Next he told her he would ask her exactly the same questions the anchor would ask in a few moments and he asked her to try to make this perfect even though it was a dry run. He then put an earpiece in her right ear and had her look slightly to the right so it wouldn't show. He told her she'll be fine and will survive the interview. She took a deep breath. She wasn't overly nervous. She had given sales pitches for years to people in make-or-break situations. This was no more difficult than that. She had been on closed circuit TV before for pitches to audiences within one company to its sites across the nation and around the world. And she would be able to answer all their questions about her sister, Mari, easily. As he was stepping out of the tiny studio, she asked him what his name was. He reached out to shake her hand and said, "Hi, Ms. Roberts. I'm Gary Wise." He moved away from the desk to a spot she could not see. But she saw him on the display above the lens.

Gary introduced Jasmine and asked her several questions. He asked about Mari, what kind of a mother she was, if she was crazy or insane, whether she demanded a lot of attention from her husband, whether she regretted being a mother, and so on. Jasmine had no trouble answering these questions confidently and clearly. Mari was described as an ideal mom. Then he asked her, "Now, would you tell our audience why your sister was in the Nation's capital yesterday without her family?"

Jasmine remembered the instructions to pause before answering. She felt herself cringe inside. That sounded like a loaded question. She smiled slightly and her eyes grew more intense as she raised her voice slightly and spoke more slowly, "My sister is very concerned about the deterioration of our God-given rights. She was attending the *Bill of Rights Restoration* march here yesterday in an effort to bring attention to this issue. She flew in Friday and was flying home after the march, being away from home only for a day."

Then Gary added a sharpness to his voice, "Do you think she regrets her decision to come to D.C. now that she's been stabbed by a fellow passenger?"

Jasmine paused to cringe inside again, "Of course not. And I would hardly call a terrorist that stabbed my sister a '*fellow* passenger'! 'Fellow' connotes camaraderie."

Gary let slip an almost imperceptible smile. "Do you agree that better security measures could have prevented your sister from being stabbed?"

"No, not necessarily," Jazz hadn't expected to be talking about airport security. She was beginning to feel the fight or flight response: pulse quickening, her lungs aching for more air, some tingling in her now sweaty palms.

"But if the TSA had strip-searched the man, or detained him, or researched his mental state, he would not have been on the plane to stab your sister!"

"No, that's not the case. A deranged person will always find a way to hurt, maim, or kill, no matter how many searches and rules and limits are imposed. And, he could have just as easily stabbed her in the airport *before* the security checkpoint."

"And what about you? Do you have it in for the TSA because they detained you on your trip here, groped you in full public view, wanted you to strip because you refused the scanner?"

Ouch. She was in a pinch. She didn't like that the interview was now about her instead of her sister. She could not let *her* ordeal take away from her sister's reputation. She couldn't let her testimony now be that the TSA both overreached with herself yet still couldn't save her sister from being stabbed. "There must be a balance between liberty and security. As you increase security efforts, people lose their liberties. On the other hand, too much liberty and the bad guys take advantage. I suppose that if all law-abiding people could and would defend themselves and defend others from the deranged and from terrorists, someone on that plane might have stopped this guy before he stabbed my sister. But we need the freedom to defend ourselves restored, first."

With that she took a deep breath to calm herself and then got up out of her seat in the tiny studio and stormed out. She felt betrayed by the changed course of the interview. Meanwhile, the engineer switched off her camera and queued the recording of her interview so they could use it as is. Within a minute, she was all the way out of the building and had flagged down a taxi. She was going to her hotel.

As he watched her on his monitor, J.B. was impressed. She spoke with confidence and certainty. He watched as the anchor deftly wove the interview that occurred between the producer and Jasmine into the coverage as though he conducted the interview himself. Replacing the producer asking the questions was Namia, however, as though she conducted the interview in the first place. Then he watched their story, which immediately followed, of how Jasmine had been detained at the airport. Namia explained the footage of Jasmine being delayed and the scene in which she found herself simply so she could come to the studio to defend her sister. Namia then went on with images of Mari in the hospital and her distraught husband at her side. Namia explained to the anchor that Mari was a normal mom and was concerned about her country. She portrayed both sisters as victims and infused the audience's sensibilities to empathy. Then she referred to Mari's expertise and writings about George Washington and showed images of her home neighborhood. J.B. was convinced at the end of the report that this Mari was purely a victim of a heinous crime by a deranged animal. This contradicted what all the other networks were running, which ran interviews with government-salaried psychiatric experts painting Mari as the aggressor and the knifeman as a bystander.

The lounge and restaurant were situated to the left side of the main lobby. Sparkling black granite table tops, dim recessed lighting, heavy black draperies, and a sleek, linear bar awaited him as he strode in, ready for a cold beer and a meal. There, at a pub-style 4-top table adjacent to the bar, was Jasmine wearing comfortable jeans and a fluffy sweater. Her make-up was gone now and she looked fresh from the shower. She had a mug half full of unfiltered beer in front of her and a bowl of salad. She was looking up at the TV above the bar running the days' events. It was ECF News. He moved around the entryway into her field of view and asked if he could join her. She looked stunned a moment, but then with recognition, said, "Yes, of course. It's J.B., right?"

"Yes, Jasmine. How are you feeling now that the interview is over? Relieved, angry, or wanting to do some more?"

She laughed. "I think I'm feeling all three. I'm glad it's over on the one hand, I'm angry that I didn't say all I wanted to, and I'm energized to speak up again."

As he slid into the barstool across from hers, he couldn't help noticing her earrings glimmered like the quartz in the table top. He looked past her to the bar and saw there were a couple of other people leaning on it and one table on the far side with four guests eating dinner. No one seemed to recognize him and no one seemed to be watching the TV, so they were unlikely to recognize her. "I feel that way each time I'm interviewed. I guess that's why I keep volunteering to appear and be interviewed. Each time I appear I feel the need to be more precise the next time."

They chatted about her ordeal at the airport, about her sister's ordeal the previous day, about the state of the world, of government, and he answered her grilling questions about why he came to Washington to serve and that he was a PE instructor in an elementary school before his current role. She was enjoying the conversation so she hadn't thought much past the present moment. But it occurred to her, as she was smiling about his antics with the schoolchildren, that he was not only a powerful presence but also a handsome man. His eyes were smiling and his features average. She imagined he must be muscular underneath. Yes, his eyes were his best feature. Her curiosity then piqued and she looked at his hands. No ring.

He caught her looking at his hands. He spread his fingers out palms down and proclaimed, "No, I'm not a metrosexual; I don't get manicures and when I am home I work with my hands on various projects, mostly building houses."

She laughed out loud – partly from knowing she had been caught and partly from his deflection of the obvious. She held her hands out similarly to show them off and announced laughingly, "I'm not a metrosexual either. But I work in sales and my customers size up everything about me every time I make a presentation. I've found that neutral but manicured hands are the most appropriate statement I can make for my hands."

He laughed out loud then and reached across the table and touched her hand. He then said straight out, "Well, well, neither of us has a ring on. I guess that means we're both single. And in case you're curious, no, I've never been married."

She was awed by his directness. She liked it. She couldn't stop herself from joining the directness and said, "I've never been married either." Although hers was in a muted voice, choking on being so direct. And he was still touching her hand. She liked it but she didn't know what to do. So she just held still.

J.B. pulled his hands back as the waiter brought their checks. They paid up and walked to the elevators. He asked, "What time are you going to the studio tomorrow?"

"I'm not sure. I ran out of there before anyone told me when they need me back."

"Well, I'm going early, for their morning show. I usually go to the Starbucks next door for breakfast and then I enjoy walking to the studio. Would you like to join me? We could meet here in the lobby at 6:30 and arrive at the studio for make-up by 7:30."

She liked the idea of seeing him again. And she liked the low-key sound of coffee and a morning walk. She couldn't prevent the big smile she flashed as she said, "Yes, that sounds great."

She pushed the 9th floor button as she entered the elevator. He followed her in and pushed the button to the 7th floor. When the elevator slowed at the 7th floor, he leaned down close to her and whispered, "It's a date then. I'll see you at 6:30."

She couldn't remember the last time she felt like this. Interested. Curious. Dreamy. Excited. She dated a lot, but only to keep in practice, not because she was interested in the men or found them desirable. They were all the same, self-centered but directionless. Since she was 27 years old, she knew she should be dating regularly so she did so, but not because she enjoyed their company. Now that she met J.B., she felt she had met a *man*. A real man. Someone who knew what was important and did something about it. Someone who knew who he was. That was the difference. He wasn't going through the motions of life; he was really living, and with purpose.

SEVEN

Monday Morning, Camp David

The staffer sat at the desk taking in a moment of peace before the morning rush began. It was 6:00 am and it was usually busy by this time of morning with reporters, Congressmen, lobbyists, senior advisors, department officials, and others calling him with messages for the President. He had already taken 15 messages down and given the list to the Chief's first assistant, Rebecca. Rebecca made his job easier by always taking the messages without complaint. He liked working in the White House because it was always so busy. This morning, however, he was working at Camp David, as the President wasn't expected back to the White House until 7:30 a.m.

He looked up from his desk near the foyer and gazed across the living room. There, President Percival Orinthbey emerged from his bedroom suite, looking freshly showered and spunky. The phone rang and the staffer answered it. While he was taking the detailed message, his gaze was drawn across the living room again, and he saw the Secretary of State emerge from the bedroom, also looking fresh from the shower and in a new crisp business suit. She walked away toward the rear door, away from where his desk was positioned, presumably to where her car was parked. He pressed the button to Rebecca's desk. Rebecca came in to see him a moment later. He gave her the newest message. Underneath it, on its own sheet of paper, he had scribbled the gossip that POTUS had a sleepover again with Bella. Rebecca glanced at the note. She nodded to him 'a job well done'.

Awakened by the first morning light peeking through the blinds, Kale rolled off his leather couch in his office. He fell asleep in front of his wall of televisions again. The morning news was already running, along with his exercise video. His automatic coffee maker kicked on, and he grabbed an O.J. from his bar-fridge behind his desk. ECF was replaying the interview with this woman's sister. She was credible and convincing. The Brain won't be happy.

As if on cue, the phone rang, Kale answered curtly, "Yeah." He could see it was the Brain.

"Kale. Do you see what ECF is running?"

"Yes, Mr. Star. I watched it last night and I'm watching the replay right now. She's very convincing."

"Well I'm tired of hearing her. I'm going to send Bo to change her story. In the meantime I need you to find someone who will go on ECF News and tell the truth, that this woman did this to herself to get her husband's attention. Got it?"

Before Kale could respond Star hung up the phone.

When Ritalia arrived Sunday morning he set her up with her work to become Mari's best friend. They put together a script and Ritalia studied all the individuals involved. She practiced several times. Now this morning they were ready. Kale placed the call to ECF News. He had Ritalia portray herself as Mari's best friend. She explained that the sister, Jasmine, was never around and didn't know Mari like she,

Ritalia did. That the sister has a big time job and lives an hour away and is always too busy to play with her nieces and nephews. She, on the other hand, babysat for the children all the time and Mari confided in her frequently that Mari and Jake were too busy to spend any time together, since they both worked and had 4 children to attend to. She said Mari was upset with her appearance as she grew older and was visiting D.C. to meet with a plastic surgeon to fix up parts of her body and face.

Kale decided to give Ritalia a raise. She was a great actress as he listened to the ECF producer soak it all in.

Then the producer asked if Ritalia could come to the studio. She said no, her husband would not let her. She then explained that her husband forbade her from making this phone call because he wanted to retain their anonymity. She then whispered that she and her husband were in a very strict religion, that she was disobeying her husband by making the phone call; and that she could not divulge any more. So she asked that her name and her call to them be kept secret.

The producer seemed too easy at understanding this. But Kale had already ensured that when the producer researched the name and background of whom Ritalia was acting as, that all the pieces would fit. And hopefully they'd run the story.

After the phone call, Kale peeked out the window and saw the sun's first glow appear to the east. Then he turned back to the set of televisions on the wall and continued watching the news stories coming out on all the channels. He was sure the Brain would be satisfied, as they kept getting closer to the goal. He knew that Star was a megalomaniac that wanted to see how far his reach of influence went. Very far, Kale knew. Money talked. And the more Star invested, the more he reaped. The bottom line was both Star and Kale understood humanity and what motivates people. It's really easy to control the message and to take power when you can manipulate people to help you.

Kale thought back to when he first met Star almost 25 years before. Kale was a college student, an editor in the college newspaper, a member of the numerous groups, popular, friendly, outgoing, and a decent student. Star had come to the campus to meet with a group he had recently joined, 21st Century Leaders of America. They had discussed policy, action, motivation, and finance. Star wrote them a grant check right then and there, to cover 2 years of their expenses, and gave them a list of activities he wanted them to do. Seemed simple enough. Kale had led the charge, knowing that Star would continue funding him and his group if they were successful. Star did come back at the end of the two years and awarded Kale a scholarship to pay for his law school at Harvard. Kale was grateful then, but knew now he had been bought then. He resented that, because he knew he was capable of accomplishing anything he wanted to. He had. But he realized too late he was doing Star's bidding in exchange for the money. How was that different from being on the corporate dole? After all that's what they were fighting for – to take down evil, over-powerful corporations that had ruined America. And yet, Star used the same methods. Kale confronted Star a few years back. Star eased his concern by telling him "*the ends justify the means*". Kale knew this was true. We must focus on the ends, whether we like the means of getting there or not. But today, he was over it. He was 54 after all. He had spent his entire life running an entire arm of Star's organization. And now he was going to ensure the ends were achieved. Kale was tired of spending years living under Star's orders and his long-protracted effort to implement the plans. But they were almost there. Kale had to keep his eye on the ends, the utopian promise.

* * * * *

Drying her hair and observing her reflection in the mirror, Jasmine smiled to herself. She would see the Congressman in a few minutes to walk to the studio. After the morning's interviews, she would head straight back to the airport and fly home. She would only miss one day of work. She glanced at her phone – no messages yet from her clients. She had sent them emails last night explaining she was out of town for the day for family matters and expected to return to the office on Tuesday. She shut off the hair dryer and hung it back up on the wall. Then she put on her eye shadow, mascara, and lipstick. She blotted on a tissue and packed up her toiletries in her bag. She shut off the lights, grabbed her bag, and headed out the door. As she stepped into the hallway, she saw a man enter his own room at the far end of the hall. She thought it was odd someone else was awake and fully dressed like her, but was heading *back* into his room. She shrugged it off. She walked to the center of the hall and pressed the call button for the elevator. The door opened and she stepped in. As the doors were closing she realized someone was rapidly approaching her elevator. She didn't bother pressing the "Door Open" button because it was too late and there would be another elevator soon without much traffic yet this morning. She glanced at her watch. Right on time.

The elevator slowed to a stop and the doors slid open. She stepped into the lobby and saw it was already starting to bustle. Three different groups of people were assembling in the lobby, dressed in business suits. Pastries were arranged on a table with a coffee pot and thick paper cups. She looked to her right and there was J.B. looking handsome and crisp. He gave her a huge smile that melted her knees as he walked toward her. He reached out to her and she wasn't sure why. Then he grabbed the back of her right elbow and swiftly led her through the lobby and out the main door. They turned left on the sidewalk to head to the Starbucks, which was 100 yards away. Though the sun was barely glowing, the streets were well lit with lamps and car headlights. It was very cool this morning and she wished she already had her coat on. J.B.'s coat was hanging over his left arm, the one holding her elbow. That spot was the only warm spot left on her body by the time they entered the coffee shop. But it was warm and welcoming inside. Several people were sitting at the tiny tables inside, staring at laptops and other electronic devices while sipping lattes and eating scones. No one looked up at them as they entered. Four people were working behind the counter already, two baristas and two cashiers. J.B. stepped up to the counter and then looked at Jasmine. She spoke clearly and directly to the young, handsome man behind the counter. "I would like a venti peppermint mocha, non fat, light whip." J.B. ordered a grande caramel macchiato, no whip. He turned to her,

"What will you have to eat? Pumpkin bread?"

"Sure, that sounds good."

"And two slices of pumpkin bread" he said to the server. As he paid for their order the other server handed Jasmine two plates. She moved to a small two-top table by the front window. She sat down and J.B. sat after pocketing his change. As they sat eating, many people were coming and going. But one man was sitting at a table outside on the sidewalk. Jasmine saw him sitting there.

"That guy must be cold. And he doesn't have a coffee to keep warm."

J.B. turned to look outside. "Yes. That is kind of weird, isn't it?" He studied the man.

The baristas called their drinks out. Jasmine jumped up, "I'll get them – you sit."

She stepped up to the counter and could feel J.B.'s eyes on her. She slowed her pace as she turned around and returned to the table. She placed the drinks on the table and then sat down. She saw someone else standing near the guy outside. He didn't have a hot drink either. And he looked cold. He wasn't wearing but a sport coat.

"Look, there's another cold fellow outside."

J.B. turned back and saw the second man. He returned to his pumpkin bread and slowly ate it. Jasmine finished hers and was working on her peppermint mocha.

They spent 15 minutes inside the coffee shop and the two men remained outside their door without a drink. Finally, J.B. stood up and went to the counter to speak with the manager of the Starbucks. He leaned over and asked, "So you let people sit at your tables out there even if they're not consuming your drinks?"

She leaned back and said, "You know, that almost never happens. And if it does, it's usually an obvious vagrant. Most people come in and get at least a shot of espresso, especially on a cold day like today."

J.B. came back to the table. He looked out the window again and then back at Jasmine. "You know, it is awfully cold this morning. We could take a taxi to the studio. And with the time we allotted ourselves, we could wait here the 15 minutes it would take for a taxi to get here."

Jasmine thought a warm taxi would be preferred over the brisk walk. "How far is it to walk?"

"About 15 minutes, just under a mile."

"We can handle that. Or if we do get a taxi, we can go back to the hotel to the taxi stand by the lobby."

She had a point, he thought. Why call a taxi when one was just down the road. Even then, it's not that far to walk. But he didn't like these two guys hanging around. "Okay. We'll walk. But let's go out the back door. The studio is that direction and it will save us 20 yards out in the cold weather."

She laughed. "Fine."

They stood up, put on their coats, and put their trash in the containers. As they did so, the guy sitting at the table outside stood up. Now J.B. thought that was too much of a coincidence. He quickly texted the D.C. police to alert them his location and his warning code. That put his phone into a recording mode and sent a signal of its location back to the D.C. police headquarters. Ever since the number of threats on members of Congress increased dramatically in the recent years, the D.C. police put together a set of codes for representatives to text to them, the messages of which automatically included their GPS coordinates. J.B. never used it before but he had attended all the practice drills the police offered to Congress and its staffers to keep the codes fresh in their minds. Now he was glad he knew what to do. Because those guys were too suspicious to ignore.

J.B. turned around the counter and said over his shoulder to the staff, "Have a great day."

The manager called back to him, "You, too, Congressman!"

Jasmine blushed realizing that everyone there knew whom J.B. was and that she was *with* him. Then she felt that was okay with her. She put a skip in her step as they walked out into the cold air.

Marine One was waiting outside the door of Camp David. Rebecca brought the President's briefcase to the helicopter, climbed into the back seat and set it beside her. About 10 minutes later the President emerged from the door and walked across the frost-browned-grass and climbed into the chopper. The pilot paid no mind to the President's big smiles this morning, even as he commented it was a hot and delicious morning. "Yes, Mr. President," was the benign response.

Rebecca handed Orinthbey several hard-covered folders and a pen. Each one had a small yellow-sticky tape with an arrow on it that read "Sign Here". He scratched his name on each, about 20 in all, as the pilot readied to lift off. He handed them back to her and asked what time Blake was coming to meet with him. She checked her watch. "Blake should be arriving when we land."

"Good. Make him wait in the outer lobby for 20 minutes. I want you to personally get him his coffee and some Danish.

I want you to chat him up for a while and find out what you can about what's happening on the Hill and write me a brief before lunch. Okay?"

"Yes, Mr. President."

"What calls do I need to make this morning?"

"There are about 2 dozen on the docket. Would you like to see the list?"

"Nah. Are there any that VP can handle?"

"Sure. Do you want to pick them?"

"Nope. Don't have time. You sort them and show me which I'm making and which she's making."

"Yes, Mr. President."

"What meetings do we have planned today?"

"After Blake at 7:30, you have National Security briefing at 8, nothing until 2 lunch meetings, one with the Senate Majority Leader and one with the Mexican Foreign Minister. And after three awards events in the Oval office this afternoon, you will speak on National TV at 7pm, well before Monday Night Football."

"When do I travel to New York?"

"You are supposed to leave tonight after your remarks. Then you are scheduled to meet with the Governor at 9pm and tour three plants in the morning, at 9, 10, and 11am. Then you'll head back here at noon to have lunch with dignitaries from Israel."

By this time, Marine One was landing on the White House lawn. There were about 40 members of the press assembled awaiting his arrival. He glanced in the mirror on the back of the pilot's seat in front of him and saw he looked perfect. "Good enough," he called back to Rebecca.

Upon landing, a Marine opened his door and stood at its side. He emerged from his seat, stood tall, and saluted the Marine. Then he waved to the press and walked briskly toward the door. He heard several members of the press call out. He waved and smiled but didn't respond.

EIGHT
Monday Morning, Crystal City Coffee Shop

As they approached the sidewalk at the end of the block, J.B. felt the hairs on his neck tingle. He realized there were no people around. Not a good place to be, he thought.

Just then an old van pulled up to the traffic light at the corner they were approaching. Jasmine saw the man in the passenger seat and stepped back in fright. J.B. grabbed her arm then and pulled her back. They turned to head back to the coffee shop but the two goons who were waiting at the table outside were now in front of them walking slowly and menacingly toward them. J.B. spoke up, "What is this about? Let us through" he demanded. The man in front, the one who had been sitting outside the coffee shop responded, "Get in the van. We just want to talk." Jasmine turned to look behind them. There were two men that had stepped out of the van – now four men surrounding them. She reached for the outside pocket of her handbag, grabbed the 4 inch-long device, felt for the trigger, aimed, and sprayed the man immediately in front of her with pepper spray. He yelled, "You stupid bitch!" Jasmine screamed loudly and shrilly for help and even J.B. was stunned by the sound she made. The man in front grabbed her arm and pushed her into the open door of the van. He knew J.B. would follow. And he did.

The second guy strapped J.B.'s hands together behind his back. Jasmine kicked and screamed. At that, the first guy shoved a towel into her mouth; the unsprayed-man from the van picked her up in a grip she couldn't free herself from. And the first guy from the coffee shop shook his head wondering why she was fighting so hard.

Inside the windowless, dark van Jasmine's feet were stuck into some containers. She couldn't move them or lift her feet. Her hands were now tied in front of her and she still had a towel stuck in her face. Her hair was loosely flying all around her. J.B.'s feet were also stuck into some containers while his hands remained behind his back. He knew the D.C. police would follow the signal on his phone and discover this creepy looking van. It wouldn't be long before they were rescued.

First guy said, "Look. Just listen. All we got is a message to deliver to her" as he cocked his head in Jasmine's direction. He looked at her now. "You got to get your story straight about this sister of yours. We know she's making it up. We know she's trying to get attention. You got to stop buttin' in to the news business, 'cause you ain't got no business in the news business. You listenin'? Now we know where you work, we know who your friends are, we know where you live, what you drive, we know who's takin' care of your nieces and nephews. Unde-stand what I mean?" he slurred.

Jasmine felt cold. She felt pins and needles in the palms of her hands. Her heart was pounding. Her head was pounding. Not only was she being threatened into lying about her sister. But they were threatening the children. She didn't care what happened to her. But she did care about them. They were innocent. She listened to everything he said, how he said it, what he was wearing, what the inside of the van looked like. She saw the driver and the three other guys, one still blotting his eyes of the tears caused by her dead-on hit with pepper spray.

First guy reached over to pull the towel out of her mouth. He had a look on his face that was still asking if she understood.

As the towel came out, she nodded her head sideways to motion him closer. He couldn't prevent himself from obeying her gesture. Just then she spit right into his eye with the wad of saliva and mucous that had accumulated in her mouth. As he blinked in stunned disbelief, she head-butted him on the chin.

"Damn you" he shouted back to her and backhanded her left eye. J.B. was wriggling to get free to help her. He couldn't believe how gutsy she was.

First guy screamed at the driver in a foreign language. He yanked the steering wheel sharply to the right and bounced off the curb. The fourth guy slid the door open to the van, and both Jasmine and J.B. were shoved out of the van door and onto the sidewalk. As soon as their bucketed-feet were clear of the van, the driver squealed the wheels and took off.

Jasmine's shoulder hurt the worst. She had landed on it on the side of the curb as they were dumped out. J.B. hit backside first and wasn't too damaged. But neither of them could lift their feet out of the street. In the light of the morning they could see that the bad guys had shoved their feet into some buckets of cement that was hardening rapidly. Their feet weighed them down so heavily they couldn't drag them out of the gutter onto the sidewalk, nor could they stand up or even sit up.

Some passers-by came running up. One was already calling 9-1-1. Another was snapping pictures of the van as it drove off. Then snapping pictures of the victims.

Jasmine just laid there feeling the shock come over her. The trauma was over. A boy, or was it a young man, stood over her. "Ma'am. Can you hear me? I'm going to lift your head." She blinked in response. She felt herself start to tremble. He put his coat over her to keep her warm. He started gently asking her questions, "What day is it?", "Where were you going?", "Do you live near here?", "What did you eat for breakfast?" She focused on his voice as she closed her eyes. She mumbled her answers back to him.

Sirens started wailing louder and louder. Jazz looked up and saw dark brown hair. The mouth was moving on the face. It was the young man speaking. He said the ambulance had arrived and the police were there, too. He said he would stay with her. She mouthed, "Where is J.B?" He replied, "He's about 5 feet away from you. The D.C. police are talking with him. He looks fine." A heavy blanket was placed on her legs. She felt herself get calmer and the shaking stopped.

Then she could hear voices above her. The young man holding her head up was saying, "She was going into shock. So I elevated her head, put my coat on her, and talked with her."

"Any loss of consciousness?"

"No."

"Any signs of bleeding?"

"Not that I could see."

"Any broken bones?"

"I think she landed on her shoulder. I saw them dump her out of the van onto the street. She went head first. And I think she said her shoulder hurt when I first came up to help her."

"Good work. You can see the police officer now. I'm sure they'll want to talk with you."

She couldn't get her mouth and voice to work. She wanted to tell him not to go, to thank him for helping, to ask his name. But her voice couldn't be found. But she felt him squeeze her arm and wish her well. She did try to smile then as she flicked her eyes.

J.B. was sitting up now. He was shaking his head in disbelief. The police sergeant was standing over him apologizing they didn't arrive sooner. He explained that

Virginia isn't part of their jurisdiction. They got the call and were on it immediately. But the local police were not part of their system and didn't put a priority on the D.C. police's call. The D.C. police headed down straight away but they were several minutes away.

Just then a fire truck pulled up and three big fellows jumped down. They saw the metal pails of cement around the Congressman's feet and got to work with a saw to cut the cement away. J.B. didn't like the look of their tools so close to his feet. But he wondered what alternative they'd have. Then he saw a blow torch get fired up. He decided to ask for one of their fire-proof coats and he'd look the other way. As he looked behind him he saw that Jazz was being tended to by 3 different EMTs, 2 police officers, and her young fellow was still standing by to look over her. J.B. asked the sergeant to thank the boy for looking after Jasmine.

Percival stepped out of the Oval Office and gave a warm welcome to Congressman Blake, "Honorable Reggie, how is it going?"

Reginald Blake was a short, stout, crotchety old man that served in Congress for 40 years. He didn't like these whipper-snapper young, inexperienced Presidents coming and going and acting all superior to him. He held the reins of power in Washington because he held the purse strings. So these young leaders of the free world had to beg him for the money for their do-goodies. While he was still in the reception area in front of several staffers, he tried to force a smile and said, "Good morning, Mr. President," his voice scratchy and cackly from a worn voice box. Percival ushered him into the open door and closed it quietly behind him.

Blake handed him a thick folder with 3 separators, "Here is the bill. Here is a set of prepared remarks you should use in your speech tonight. Here are the questions the Press will ask you about this and here are the answers. We're going to review this in committee this week. It will pass on a party-line vote. It will go to the full House next week. It may have some trouble there. Here is a list of names of members of the House that will likely resist this. Here are their bios, personal info, their concerns, and how you can counter each one, some by argument and some by arm-twisting, and some by buying off with these other bills that are important to them. It's all there, everything you need to get this done. Got any questions?"

Blake drummed his fingers impatiently waiting while Percival thumbed through the packet Blake gave him. Orinthbey was still amazed at the power of the army of staffers on the Hill to compose and execute perfect orchestrations of the legislative process.

"This looks great," Percival vocalized meekly. He couldn't think of anything that was missing or wrong about the packet.

"Good. Call me if you need anything. And don't f#*k this up." Blake left without a nod or a good-bye. There was no attempt at civil niceties until he opened the door to the reception area full of staff members. "Thank you, Mr. President," he called back into the room.

Percival sat at his desk shaking his head slightly. What did it mean to be President when you were just a figure-head that others pushed around, the ones that thought they ran the place?

He looked at his watch, 7:50. Good, he thought. He'd see Bella at the Briefing in a few minutes. That was the bright spot in his day. And he had nothing scheduled until his first lunch meeting at 11 a.m. He forgot about Blake and was again happy about his day.

At 10:55 Rebecca looked up from her workstation to see Secretary of State Bella Gliad slip out of the Oval Office. She had been in there for 2 hours. Bella walked right up to Rebecca's desk and asked for messages. Rebecca blushed for a moment. "Yes, you have one. Your assistant said that you need to get back to State ASAP because a situation is brewing in the Republic of Indonesia. He wanted the official position because their Foreign Minister is asking for help to quell some protests."

"Ok. Thanks." She took the message and swirled around in her heels and headed down the hall.

Rebecca pulled out her notebook from her purse and made a note of the time.

Later Jasmine and J.B. were fixed up at the Virginia Hospital Center after the fire department removed the cemented feet buckets. Jasmine's shoulder was x-rayed and found to be just bruised. The few minor scrapes were cleaned up and glued shut. Pain relievers were used for the soreness. Police statements were issued. The D.C. police were looking for the van and reviewing the footage from J.B.'s camera. There were promises of finding the perpetrators. Then Jasmine said she wanted a police detail on her sister's home. She reminded the police that these guys threatened her nieces and nephews hundreds of miles away.

It was nearly noon by the time the ordeal was over. J.B. had called his office earlier and they sent a car to pick him up. As they walked out of the hospital he asked her to join him in the car. She didn't argue. She climbed in and he asked her whether she wanted to go to the ECF studio, or to the airport, or to his local apartment to rest, or to his office with him. She said, "Let's go to the studio. That's why I spent the night here last night and that's one way to let those goons know they can't threaten me into doing what they want." He told his driver where to take them and watched as she called her parents to let them know what was happening and to be on alert. Then she called Jake and updated him, too.

Jake answered, "Hi Jasmine. Thanks for getting me the news through Mom and Dad."

"Jake. You are not going to believe what's been happening. But first tell me how Mari is."

"She's doing better. They still have her on a lot of pain medicine; they're draining her stomach through the wound. But she's been labeled as stable condition, believe it or not."

"Good. That's good to hear. Look, Jake. I came to D.C. yesterday to speak on national news about how wonderful a mother Mari is and what she's been through. But it's been a complete mess. I went through an ordeal to get here and I just left the hospital here."

"Wait? What? You're at a hospital? Are you okay?"

"Don't worry about me. But we were kidnapped and threatened by these goons who want me to tell the world that Mari is disturbed and needing attention. They know you two have kids and they were threatening to hurt them if I didn't go along with their story." She told him the details of the kidnapping.

Jake's incredulity made him speechless. He thought about the psychiatrist, Dr. Hildebrand, and the car ride to the hospital. He told Jasmine about Hildebrand's remarks in the car on the way to the hospital. He let the "*we* were kidnapped" go. And he realized he could learn the details later. Now was the time to stay focused. "Did you call Mom and Dad about the kids?"

"Yes, of course. They're on the lookout."

"I can take care of Mari. We'll get out of here as soon as I can move her. Perhaps we should meet at our rendezvous?"

"Do you think this is *that* bad?"

"Jasmine, you were kidnapped. Your feet put into cement buckets. Maybe they were going to dump you into the Potomac!!!"

"Hmmm. Maybe you're right. Where did you say that doctor was from? And who sent him?"

Jake reminded Jasmine of the conversation he had had. He could hear her thinking the same thing. This was a much bigger problem than just one lone nutcase on an airplane stabbing a passenger. There was a conspiracy here of some sort. Too many people involved to kidnap her, threaten the kids, and send a psychiatrist vouching for this story to meet his airplane. "And have you been watching the news?"

"No, I haven't had a chance. What's happening?"

"Every channel is running these stories about Mari wanting attention and fabricating the whole thing."

"What? That's crazy."

"Not only that, but they got her friend Riana to vouch for the story, too, though anonymously."

"I don't believe that."

"Well if she didn't do it on purpose, she agreed with the leading questions of her interview."

"I still don't believe it. Did they show her on TV saying these things?"

"Well. No. But they described her as Mari's best friend and displayed quotes from her, supposedly."

"I'm going to call her. How much time do you need?"

"At least a day. Probably 2 or 3 days."

"Do you need me to help you?"

"I don't know yet. You take care of yourself. I'll keep you posted when I can move Mari and when I can meet you. Okay?"

"Okay. Give her a kiss for me."

NINE
Monday Midday, Crystal City, Virginia

Jasmine pondered the conversation she just had with Jake. She looked across the back seat at J.B. He was trying to politely ignore her conversation by texting his staff but when she stared at him, he looked back at her with a look of concern.

"Is your sister okay? What did the doctor say?" J.B. inquired thoughtfully.

"The doctor?"

"Yes, you asked Jake what the doctor said and who sent him. What do you mean who sent him? Wasn't he at the hospital?"

"No. Jake said that when his plane landed in Atlanta, he was taken off the plane onto the tarmac where a vehicle was waiting for him. In the car he rode with an airline representative plus a psychiatrist who told Jake that Mari was crazy. J.B., this sounds too coincidental not to be orchestrated by someone with lots of pull."

J.B. had seen many such "orchestrations" during his time in D.C. He had concluded that they weren't really

79

conspiracies by some mastermind somewhere behind the scenes but more of the flocking behavior he observed with humans – they all flew the same direction whether they meant to or not. So to him it was possible that the doctor was legitimate, was in denial that a crazed man would attack an innocent woman, had seen too many cases of overworked moms demanding attention in such ways, and came to this conclusion independently of the goons that kidnapped them hours before. The goons were just goons and were protecting some belief of their own using the means at their own disposal. "We shouldn't jump to any conclusions. At the moment there is no evidence that the psychiatrist and the goons are operating at the behest of some 'mastermind'. Do you agree?"

Jasmine had to agree that this was true. "Ok. We'll wait to conclude they're in cahoots until we know more. In the meantime, I need to get ready for an interview. Are you going on the air this morning, too?"

"Well, like you, that was my plan, that's why I stayed overnight near the studio, too. So let's do it."

The car had arrived at the studio and was idling in the portico while Jasmine and J.B. finished their conversation. Jasmine went to grab the door handle when J.B. reached over to stop her. "Jazz, let me drive you from ECF studios when we're done today – to the airport, the hotel, wherever you are ready to go, please wait for me. Yesterday you ran out of here without saying good-bye to me and I don't want that to happen again today, okay?"

She couldn't help but smile. "Okay."

He jumped out of the car to open her door. She let him. She was still sore and achy in her feet and shoulder. So she appreciated his attentiveness. They walked up to the grand rotating front door entrance to the studio and were greeted by a lovely, bright-faced liaison who recognized them both and brought them into the bowels of the studio complex and to the make-up room.

* * * * *

After the interview, Jasmine returned to the studio's lounge adjacent to the makeup room to wait for J.B. Now starving, she ate some of the cheese, crackers, and grapes they had left out on a table along with bottles of water and apple juice. She felt safe in the studio and didn't want to ponder the possibility of being kidnapped again by goons following this interview. She recalled the pain she felt when the makeup person tried to cover the scrape on her left cheekbone from the goon smacking her across the face. Jazz decided then to have it show through. During her interview, this time live on the set with Namia, she described in detail the kidnapping, the descriptions of the goons, the vehicle they were driving, and everything they said. She made a plea to the audience to find the culprits and get them off the streets. Jasmine assured the audience she would press charges and testify against these men. Namia had asked her to speculate on whom they could be but Jasmine wasn't falling for it. She deflected Namia's repeated questions about them by clearly and patiently reminding Namia that she couldn't speculate why they were there, whom they might know, nor why it was so important to them that she lie about Mari.

She looked up at the TV suspended from the ceiling and saw J.B. wrapping up his interview with the anchor. After he had finished discussing legislative proposals about transportation security, he directed the conversation to the rights of individuals to speak freely, to come onto ECF News to tell about their sister's state of mind, to describe a crime that had taken place, and to not be intimidated by people that use violence or even coercion to stop others from speaking freely. He pointed out that freedom of speech is a most basic human right, a God-given right, and deserves protection.

A few moments later, J.B. strolled into the lounge. He made a bee-line to the table with the snacks and grabbed an apple juice and some cheese and crackers on a plate. He sat down across from her and ate. Then he asked her, "Where to? Are you going to the airport to go home or are you staying here?"

She hadn't wanted to think about her next step. Her mission here was completed. She needed to rendezvous with Mari and Jake and her parents and the children. But it occurred to her that it might be the last she saw of J.B. "Yes, I suppose I need to head home. But…" she paused a long time. He waited. "…I don't think I'm ready to say 'good-bye' to you."

He laughed and she felt more at ease. She wasn't accustomed to speaking frankly. She never had before. "Well, I'm not sure I'm ready to say 'good-bye' either. But I have work to do and you work, too, don't you?"

"Well yes, I do. I'm in sales and my boss let me have today off but I had told him I'd be back tomorrow."

"Then you mustn't keep him waiting. We should meet somewhere this coming weekend so we can see each other again"

She hadn't conceived of dating or seeing him again, given that they lived in different states. This would not be easy. "Do you like to go fishing or kayaking?"

He gave her a surprised look. "I should have known you're an outdoorsy girl by the way you handled those goons."

"Yes, I am. Tell you what. I'll stay here until late tonight. I'll fly back on a 9 or 10pm flight. And if you have time to spend with me, I'll spend the rest of the day with you. Then we can decide whether to try to see each other this coming weekend. Does that work?" She regretted the strictly-business sounding tone but she couldn't help it. Business conversations were her comfort zone; speaking to a handsome man that she was attracted to about possibly taking the next step in beginning a relationship was not.

"I find your suggestion agreeable," he replied in a business-contract-making tone.

She laughed at that. He stood up, leaned closer to her, and put his hand out for her to take. She placed her hand in his. He gave it a slight squeeze and she stood up close to him. She could feel his strength now and it made her a bit weak.

They were silent as they walked through the lobby, out the rotating door, across the portico, and into his car. He told the driver to head west. Then he leaned over and whispered to her, "I was so impressed with how you fought back against those guys. But I want you to always win, to never lose when fighting bad guys. Would you like to learn more self-defense?"

"My Dad always emphasized being able to protect ourselves. I guess I learned to be tough from him. What did you have in mind?"

"I know this guy who runs a shooting range in Falls Church. We could go use the range and if he has time he can show us some moves."

"Sure. That sounds like a fun date." She giggled. He laughed, too, and told the driver the address.

Along the ride, they both were busy making phone calls, responding to emails and text messages. When they arrived at the shooting range J.B.'s friend Mike was standing in the parking lot waiting for them.

"Hey, J.B., it's been a while" Mike called to them as they exited the car.

"There isn't enough downtime. The Nation's business keeps me busy around the clock."

Mike studied their appearance as they approached. "So what exactly happened to you two?"

J.B. told Mike they came to take a quick class in self-defense since they were kidnapped that morning. He retold some of the details. Mike escorted them around to the rear entrance where they would have some privacy from the other customers. He sat them down in a small office. And he asked Jasmine, "Have you ever handled firearms before?"

Jasmine took a deep breath. "When I was a teenager my Dad took me to the range to shoot clay pigeons with the 12 gauge. And the best times I had talking with my Dad were when he was cleaning his handguns on the patio."

"That's good" acknowledged Mike.

"My Dad always wanted me to take up shooting sports. He would go to all these competitions on weekends and he was a member of a club that met once per week. But I was always too busy with gymnastics, cheerleading, student government, drama club, and 4H."

"I think it's important to know that a firearm is a tool. Think of a fire extinguisher in your home, office, or public building. We have them just in case there is a fire, although we hope and expect never to have to use the fire extinguisher to put out a fire. The same is true for using or carrying a firearm for self defense. We carry the tool with us in case we need it, but we never expect to need to use it."

Jazz nodded her head and looked at J.B. He already knew this apparently.

Mike continued, "It doesn't make us a bad person to keep a fire extinguisher in our cars and homes. It makes us responsible people to protect ourselves, people near us, and our property from the devastating effects of fire. But it also makes sense to be familiar with how to use a fire extinguisher beforehand so it can be used safely and effectively in a real emergency."

Jasmine was pondering this. Of course a fire extinguisher was a good thing to have. Yes, it made sense to know how to use it first. But she couldn't remember anyone she knew ever needing to use one.

He went on, "Many people carry firearms on their persons for self-defense. You'd be amazed how many do. But concealed carry is just that, concealed. The sheeple are completely unaware."

"The sheeple?" she asked.

"Yes, that's what we call the people that blindly believe they don't need to protect themselves and that the police or authorities can keep them safe."

"Well our society is pretty safe, isn't it?"

"Yes, but is that because bad guys know that when they enter a coffee shop up to one in ten customers is carrying a firearm? Forty percent of all Americans own a firearm. There are 70% more firearms in this country than people! Believe me, though the sheeple don't know how many firearms there are, the bad guys do."

Jasmine noticed how enthusiastic Mike was about sharing these facts. "But there is no way of knowing the gun possession statistics of the bad guys. They won't tell!"

"No, but you can bet that they can find a way to own guns."

She opened her mind to imagine the possibilities.

He continued, "I've studied gun facts for a long time. A fact I think is troubling is that whites are twice as likely as blacks to own guns when you look back at the Civil Rights movement. It wasn't that long ago when blacks weren't allowed to own guns at all. Guns were essential to preventing the KKK from inflicting more terror on blacks in the south. Anyway, let's get back to what we're here for now."

Mike pointed to an NRA chart on the wall behind his desk. He explained to Jasmine that there are three gun safety rules. "First, never point the muzzle of the gun at anything you are not willing to destroy. This is also known as pointing the muzzle in a safe direction." He drew her eye to the muzzle. "This wall behind my desk is made of reinforced concrete block. If a gun accidentally discharges in this direction, it won't hurt anyone." She looked at the wall. "Second, keep your finger off the trigger until you are ready to shoot. If the trigger isn't pulled, it can't go off, right?"

"Yes, that's right," she responded.

"And third, keep the gun unloaded until you are ready to use it." He looked at her to see if she got this. "Related to this, we treat every gun as though it is loaded until we prove to ourselves that it is not loaded." He paused and then continued, "In the old days, the children grew up treating all guns as loaded because they *were*. The bears, coyotes, and intruders were not going to wait for the Farmer to load his shotgun before they attacked the farm animals or entered the unlocked farmhouse."

Jasmine could feel herself filling with inspiration to learn all about firearms, their history, and data about ownership and usage. She couldn't wait to take this on as a new hobby and call her Dad with the news. She smiled with eager anticipation to learn more.

She focused on Mike's words, "Now when we handle firearms here in my office, this line, at the edge of my desk, serves as the range line. All muzzles point toward that wall," he said while pointing behind him. "And the muzzle is placed on the table toward that wall or aimed toward that wall. Do you understand?"

Jasmine nodded. The shotgun ranges she used growing up didn't really have a line. But the front of the launching machines served as the line when shooting skeet. Mike proceeded to show Jasmine an unloaded Smith & Wesson Model 60 Ladysmith .38 Special Revolver. He showed her that it was unloaded. He placed it on the carpet mat on his desk, with the muzzle facing the wall, and asked her to pick it up and point it toward the back wall. He asked her how it felt in her hand.

"It feels okay," she replied.

"Now I want you to try to cock the hammer back. Revolvers come in single action or double action. Single action revolvers require the shooter to cock the hammer back for every shot. But it's fairly easy to pull the trigger when you do. Double action revolvers will cock the hammer for you once you shoot, but the trigger takes much more finger strength pull. Some ladies don't have the strength to pull that trigger in double action mode. And if they do, they may not have the strength to pull the trigger five times in a row to unload the entire cylinder."

She tried to cock it with her thumb. "Should I pull the trigger?"

"Yes," he replied. "It's not loaded."

She pulled the trigger. She felt her confidence building as she handled her first handgun.

He explained that revolvers like the Ladysmith can only hold 5 bullets before they have to be reloaded. He showed her how to reload the revolver with dummy cartridges. "It takes a lot of time to reload. And if a petite woman like yourself is surrounded by 5 bad guys, like you were earlier today, you'd have to hit each one with exactly one bullet before they charge you with this gun in order to protect yourself from being kidnapped or worse. In other words, they're going to win if you are carrying this revolver. What if one of your bullets misses completely? Or what if you inflict just a minor flesh wound, you're just going to make the bad guys angrier and more likely to do horrible things to you once they catch you. So most people opt for a semi-automatic pistol like this," he showed her a Glock 17 semi-automatic pistol, which he placed on the carpet mat on his desk.

"The cool thing about a semi-automatic is that it cycles the action automatically: Squeezing the trigger causes the hammer to ignite the primer, causing a mini-explosion inside the cartridge. The expanding gas of the explosion pushes the bullet down the barrel and out the muzzle. Of course, there is also an opposing recoil force or "kick". It's basic physics: In a revolver the recoil force does nothing but make the gun jump. Semi–auto pistols take advantage of the recoil force to eject the spent cartridge while at the same time compressing a spring and setting up the firing mechanism for the next shot. The spring pushes the slide forward which strips a new cartridge from the magazine and chambers it into the breach so it's ready to shoot again. This all happens with in a fraction of a second so you can make follow up shots much more rapidly." He showed her how to use the slide of the gun. He showed her how the backward energy would push the slide back and the spring inside the frame would push the slide forward again. He next explained how much time transpires between shots fired on this gun versus the revolver in single-action mode. "That makes sense," she agreed. She was taking it all in.

Then Mike showed her the magazine that comes with the Glock 17. "It's a 17 cartridge magazine." He did the math for her, "If you have 5 bad guys and a 17 round magazine, you have 3 shots per dude plus two to spare. That way if you miss, graze a shoulder, you could still get him with a third shot. Now if there are 8 bad guys, you'll only have two bullets per bad guy plus a spare." He looked at her intently to see if she understood. Then he continued, "So you also need to know a 9mm round won't kill a person unless it strikes in a few very small places and at very close range. What kills a person is *force*, which is due to both the rapid deceleration of the bullet and its mass. A 9mm bullet doesn't have a lot of mass. And depending on what strength powder is in the cartridge affects its initial velocity. Once ejected from the muzzle, the bullet starts slowing down quickly from air friction. Once a bullet hits a bad guy, it decelerates rapidly. That deceleration, combined with the mass, provides the *deadly force*. More massive bullets or more velocity will result in more force. In fact, if you remember taking physics in college, you'll know that force equals mass times acceleration squared. In this case it's *deceleration* that counts."

She nodded though she hadn't studied much physics. Now she wondered what else she missed in her college courses.

"Now with a maximum of 2 bullets per bad guy, your objective is to try to kill them because more than likely you're only going to slow them down. And hopefully you won't just make them angrier while they could still inflict harm on you."

Jasmine soaked all this in. She realized all the debates from last year about magazine sizes for handguns were silly. All that could be gained by limiting *her* use of larger magazines was to make gangs add more bad guys to their group. The bad guys will just send gangs large enough to overcome the size gun she, a good guy, could carry.

She liked the sleek look of the Glock. She liked the idea of 17 bullets over 5. She dry-fired the Glock now. The trigger was much easier to pull. Mike showed her how to drop the magazine and put a new one in. She could see that it was much easier to reload the Glock.

"I want you to take a few minutes to think about what we've covered and I'll be right back," Mike said as he stepped out of the room. J.B. got up, too, and followed Mike. This gave Jasmine time to think back to their kidnapping this morning. She thought about the two men sitting outside their coffee shop in the cold. She imagined the entire scene over again had she been armed. She and J.B. had walked out the back door and intersected with the van near the corner. She could have put her hand on a holster then. And when she found them to have been surrounded, she could have aimed a gun at the thugs rather than her pepper spray. One well-placed bullet might have scared them all away. Or it may have made them act more quickly. She would have to be ready. She would have to be willing to shoot the guy she peppered, and shoot the guy next to him at the van. But the guys behind her might have jumped her during this. She would have to be able to turn around and shoot them, too? Hmmm. How would she do that? Rely on J.B. to punch them or shoot them herself? Or shoot them from a choke hold? All these thoughts told her she had a lot to learn. A lot. Now she wished she had gone to the range with her Dad.

Mike and J.B. came back into the office and Mike handed Jasmine some headphones and safety glasses. He escorted her into a booth in the room next to his office. It was dark, stuffy, and it smelled strange. She felt a bit claustrophobic. Mike turned on a light in the booth, which had a white-painted wood surface about elbow height. He pressed a light switch, which brought a clip toward them on a clothesline-looking thing. Mike attached a simple paper target to it and pressed the light switch again until it moved about 25 feet back away from them.

Next he showed her that the revolver was not loaded. He set it on the wood surface. And told her to pick it up, keeping the muzzle pointing toward the back wall of the range, and put it in her hand. He placed his arms around her and his hands over hers to show her where her right thumb should be, and then he placed her left hand over her right. He explained that her right hand keeps the muzzle of the gun from moving up and down and the left hand keeps the gun from moving in a left-right direction. "Using both hands," he explained, "will help you hit the target dead-on. Now keep your arms straight, almost locked at the elbows. This will keep the gun from kicking up too much after you fire. This is important so you can get your second shot off accurately and quickly." She practiced this position. "One more thing, lean forward slightly. When the backward force comes toward you, most will be absorbed by your hands and arms. But some will have to be absorbed by your legs and spine. Leaning forward slightly helps you remain stable on your feet. Now don't worry because it's not that bad and you'll get used to it quickly."

She looked to Mike for confirmation her position was good, her grip, and her hands. He asked her, "Are you ready?"

"Yes, sure." She was ready.

"Put the gun on the table and I'll show you how to load it. I'll load it first, then I'll unload it. Then I'll load and unload a second time. And then I'll supervise you loading it, unloading it, and loading it again. Then you can shoot it."

She watched him intently. It seemed straightforward. When he was done showing her twice, she took her turn loading and unloading the gun. Then she loaded one bullet, gripped the gun with both hands as he had shown her, all while pointing it down range. Finally she raised her thumb up to cock the hammer, and put her right hand back firmly in place. She aimed at the center of the target, and squeezed the trigger. The bang was louder than she expected, even with her headphones. She saw sparks coming out of the muzzle because it was so dark inside the range. She smelled the smoke from the primer, and she set the gun on the table as quickly as she could. She was amazed how far her arms came back up toward the ceiling from its kick. She hadn't expected that. But Mike was bringing the target back on its clothesline and Jasmine was thrilled to see she was in the center circle, not dead on, but in the vicinity. As she took a few moments to get over the sensations she just went through, she decided it was a thrill. A major thrill to shoot a handgun.

"Can I shoot it again?" she asked.

"Sure," Mike responded.

She loaded one bullet, cocked the hammer, checked her grip and fired. It was still really loud. She felt it in her chest bones. She smelled the gun powder again and was amazed at the brightness of the sparks shooting from the muzzle. Mike brought the target back and she saw her second bullet was within an inch of the first.

Mike told her, "This means you have precision, when you can get your shots close together. Accuracy is when they're where you are aiming while precision is when the shots are all close together in small groups."

She nodded in agreement while thinking that maybe shooting sports was her next 'thing'.

While she was reliving the experience, Mike was checking the revolver to ensure it was unloaded. He put it away in his case on the back table. He was asking her if she was ready to see the semi-automatic now. She looked at him and nodded, though a bit dreamily.

Mike pulled a Glock 17 semi-automatic pistol from his bag and placed it on the wood surface at the range line.

He explained to her, "Semi-automatic just means that once you shoot, the next cartridge is loaded into the chamber automatically, from the action of the previous bullet, so it's ready to shoot again. In other words, you don't have to rack it again each bullet. This saves time when you're fending off a gang of bad guys."

This again reminded her of the gang that had kidnapped her this morning. She replayed it another time. They didn't show any guns. But they didn't have to. They outnumbered her, they used the van, they tied her feet together and her hands together, and to get her into the van they manhandled her. She could tell the threat was there when J.B. had told them to let the two of them pass and they refused. Her pepper spray had not deterred them. Would a handgun have deterred them? If she had shot the guy with a bullet instead of pepper spray, they would still have kidnapped her and maybe taken her gun. She knew then that if she was going to carry a handgun for personal protection, she had to willing to use it, no matter what. There are no half measures. If you shoot one bad guy and then stop out of the horror of the act, then you'll likely be killed. This made her shiver.

Mike saw this, "Are you okay?"

"Yes, I'm just reliving this morning's ordeal."

"Are you ready?"

"Yes."

He showed her the magazine, which holds several cartridges. He showed her that the magazine has a spring in it that pushes the cartridges to its top so that they can be loaded one at a time into the gun's chamber. He showed her the magazine release on the gun. Then he showed her how to pull the rack back and check the chamber to make sure it's empty. He showed her how to load the magazine into the gun until it clicks into place and how to rack it. He had her demonstrate racking the gun (while empty) to see if she had the strength to do so. He saw she was muscular and he gave her a suggestion to turn her body slightly to the right to keep the muzzle pointing down range and to move the left hand over the right to rack it. He explained that this made use of the most leverage to help rack the gun.

He proceeded to load, unload, load, and unload this gun, as he had with the other gun. He then explained that after shooting and before setting the gun back on the wood table, she should drop the magazine onto the table and rack the gun a couple of times to make sure all cartridges are ejected and then to leave the rack open so it's clear to everyone that the gun is unloaded. He added she should point the empty gun's muzzle down range and pull the trigger to put the hammer down.

"Are you ready? I'll have you insert the magazine, rack the gun to chamber a cartridge, and then unload the magazine, and rack it until you're sure the gun is empty of ammunition. Then you can insert the magazine again, rack it, and shoot. This time you can shoot the gun at the target until you've shot all the cartridges. You'll know when the gun is empty because the rack will stay open and back. Okay?"

"Yes, I'm ready."

She stepped up and loaded and unloaded the gun. Mike nodded at her. Then she loaded it again. He checked her hands one last time to make sure her right hand fit the grip of the gun properly and that both hands were well below the rack. Then he nodded to her that it was okay to shoot.

She aimed and squeezed the trigger. This was loud like the other gun. There were sparks from the muzzle again. She didn't notice the smell of gun powder this time. And though she braced herself from the energy of the gun, it didn't seem to have as much kick as the revolver. She wasn't sure if that was because she was already getting used to shooting or if it was because the semi-automatic didn't kick as much. She squeezed the trigger again. And again. And after a few minutes she went to squeeze the trigger and nothing happened. That's when she looked and saw that the rack was back and she must be out of bullets. She dropped the magazine and set the gun on the wood table at the range line.

She stepped back out of the booth and looked at J.B., who had been standing behind her the entire time. He gave her a huge smile and said, "Well, how does it feel?"

"I love it," was all she could say.

"A great feeling of power, isn't it?"

"Yes, it's a powerful experience. It's exhilarating for me to try new things, too."

"So which gun did you like better?"

"I like the semi-automatic. More rounds can be loaded, and it seems simpler to operate. Plus the kick didn't seem as bad."

"Semi-automatics are the most popular. I have a Smith & Wesson that is similar to the Glock you fired. Now the kick has to do with the barrel length and mass of the gun. The Glock has a longer barrel so it doesn't kick as much. It's harder to conceal a gun with a long barrel but you have better aim and less kick."

She pondered this. "Sounds like I need two guns. One with a smaller barrel for concealed carry and one with a bigger barrel for my nightstand."

"I like this girl," Mike said to J.B. while giving a wink. Mike put all his gear away and said, "It won't be long before even two guns aren't enough. Most of us that get into shooting sports find we need multiple handguns depending on what we're wearing, whether we're shooting in competitions, or using one for home defense. Then we have rifles which are just plain fun to shoot, and you said you like shooting skeet, well then you have to have a shotgun, too."

She laughed at this. She didn't like to spend a lot of money but she did like being well equipped for new hobbies and decided target shooting would be a new hobby for her. She thought about her budget and what she was willing to spend on this. Her kayak and related gear cost her $1200 last year. She figured she could budget $1200 now.

"What can I be outfitted with for a maximum $1200 budget?"

Mike liked this girl. "We'll get you a great set up for $1200."

They finished up at his range and headed back to the car. J.B. had purchased a book for her on the gun laws of various states and the rules about transporting firearms. She started reading it as they got back into the car.

TEN

Monday Afternoon, Approaching the Capital

As they drove from the gun range east toward the airport, J.B.'s phone rang.

"Yeah."

"Congressman Stanton?"

"Yes, who is this?"

"My name is Dr. Hildebrand. I'm a psychiatrist from Johns Hopkins. I heard that you and Ms. Jasmine Roberts were in a bit of a scuffle today. I was hoping I could interview you both about your experience."

J.B. was curious. How did this guy know about this? "Really? Well I need to know how you knew to reach me and why you are interested." J.B. used a serious tone that was not generous.

"Of course, I understand your trepidation. I've been hired by DHS to ensure the public safety. They alerted me that you were involved this morning in an alleged kidnapping."

"It wasn't alleged." J.B. was cool. He didn't like the sound of DHS bringing some guy in, using the word alleged, and not contacting him themselves.

"Of course, of course. We're trying to develop a profile of the experiences of victims and the actions of their attackers and that's why we'd like to meet with you."

"Look. I've already filed a police report; you may read it."

"Well, I already have. But I'd like a better description of the motives of all involved."

"Sorry, but I'm not a lab rat. I don't know who you are or why you're called in and I can't support your work until I'm clear of its aim."

Now Jasmine was looking at J.B. with deep concern. She didn't like the sound of his voice; it was alarmed.

"I could explain that to you after our interview. However, scientists don't want to sway or bias the perceptions of people with the nature of their study. It's well known that people will change their stories to confirm scientists' expectations. So I cannot tell you until after the fact. I assure you our objectives are to help the government provide a worry-free environment for the traveling public."

J.B. pondered this. The guy said 'traveling public'. As a member of the transportation committee, he felt it was his responsibility to ensure that systems were in place to make travel safe. He wondered why the DHS had not briefed the Transportation Committee on the 'research' this guy was purporting to conduct. "I'll tell you what. Give me your number and I'll have a member of my staff call you later today or tomorrow to schedule an appointment next week. I know my schedule is full this week and as you can guess, today has been ruined by this morning's unexpected interference."

There was a long pause. J.B. thought he heard whispering. Finally, "Well, I'm afraid that won't work. Our research requires immediate recollection of the details of the event. By next week you'll have forgotten important elements of the events. It's imperative we meet today."

J.B. was done with this conversation, "I'm sorry you feel that way. Again, I don't feel the same urgency that you do about what happened this morning. Had you briefed the Transportation Committee on your project I might have sympathy for your predicament. But I don't. And you can't tell me the nature of the urgency of your project. So there is nothing more to discuss. I'm not available today. I've lost about 5 hours with this morning's interruption by a gang of marauders and I'd prefer to get back to the People's business as soon as possible. Good-bye."

Before J.B. pressed the "end" button on his phone he heard Dr. Hildebrand respond, "You'll regret this Congressman." But it was too late to respond because he had pressed the End button. He dialed the number for his office and spoke with his staffer, Maria.

"Maria. This is J.B. Find out what DHS is up to on the traveling public's safety. Some Dr. Hildebrand just called me on my private cell phone number and demanded time from me today to be interviewed by him about the kidnapping this morning. He said he was working for DHS and he said he couldn't wait, though I offered to meet with him next week. He was really put off by my response. Anyway, let me know when you find something out."

"Ok. I'm on it. When will you be back? You have 2 constituents here hoping to catch you today, Senator Harpin has called 3 times to see if he can meet with you, and we've had dozens of members of the press wanting to speak with you about this morning. It sounds like you need to issue a press release soon."

"Yes, of course. Here take this down and get it back to me when you polish it." He proceeded to provide a brief description of the morning's ordeal to be written up in a press release.

"So what was THAT all about?" Jasmine couldn't help the upset tone of voice.

"Some guy demanding an interview about this morning. Says he's working for DHS and won't tell me what he's up to."

"What did you say his name is?"

"Dr. Hildebrand."

Her skin turned pale and she looked like frost on a window.

"Wha-a-at?" J.B. slowly released from his mouth.

Jasmine muttered, "I can't believe this, J.B. That's the name of the doctor that Jake told me met him at the airport in Atlanta on Saturday night. That's the psychiatrist that tried to convince him that Mari was the perpetrator and not the victim. This *could* all be orchestrated!"

Now it was J.B.'s turn to feel the cold, ill feeling of something being terribly wrong in the world. "No way," he muttered to himself. He wasn't sure what to do next or where to turn for answers. He ran it all through his head. He decided the best place was to call his friend and mentor. He dialed the number.

"Ray, it's J.B. Call me back as soon as you can. Something weird is going on. Something dreadful. Something you definitely will want to know about." He decided to send a text to Ray, too. It read "call me ASAP re UWTK."

Jasmine was looking over his shoulder. Because of the fear he was exhibiting, she wanted to be close to him physically to both comfort him and be comforted by him. "What is UWTK?"

"It means 'you'll want to know'."

"Oh."

He noticed her just then. He reached his arm around her in the back seat both to comfort her and himself. She snuggled up feeling safer in the eye of doom. They enjoyed a few minutes of peace like this while the driver focused on the road ahead. She soaked this up as long as she could.

Mari woke up and blinked her eyes. Jake had been watching her and smiled at her movements. She smiled back. Though it had only been 2 days, she was recovering quickly.

She had Jake tell the nurse to stop the pain meds so she could think clearly. When she was fully awake and drinking some ice water, he decided it was time to tell her. "Mari, I think it's time for our back up plan."

"You know, Jake. I've had a lot of time to think while half asleep and half awake. I've been mulling it over in my head. I guess I've been seeing this coming for a while."

"I talked to your parents a short time ago. They have the situation under control. Because they're off today from childcare duties, they're finishing some last minute packing and preparing. I also told them how to deal with our last few items. We can be ready to go as soon as you are."

"What did the doctor say about my discharge?"

"He wants to keep you a couple more days. But I think we can convince him otherwise, since you are away from your children."

"What about Jasmine? Is she ready?"

"I'll call her next and tell her we are ready and ask her to join us. She's been through a lot, too, you know."

"Would you tell me?"

"Well, she was interviewed twice on TV to support you. But she also had a major ordeal at the airport to get to D.C. And then this morning she was briefly kidnapped by thugs that wanted her to stop speaking out in support of you."

"Oh my, is she okay?"

"She's resilient."

"Well, please call her and tell her we want her to join us as soon as she can."

A few years before as Mari was home with her young children, she started reading all sorts of books she was exposed to in a book club she had joined. It was a book club that a church member had started. She had read a fictional account of the worst case scenario where America's systems would collapse from skyrocketing inflation. That book, *Patriots*, left her with an eerie sense of doom. She started reading financial reports and watching CNBC. She made graphs and charts and collected world commodity price data. She evaluated the effects of central banks in prior instances of record inflation – the Weimar Republic, Zimbabwe, Brazil, and others – and found that the U.S. was on a dreadful course from its enormous debts and deficits. That's when she convinced her husband to start preparing for the worst case scenario, too. She watched TV shows like "The Best Defense" to learn about survival in a long term wide area catastrophe, much like Hurricane Katrina's effect in Mississippi and New Orleans. She joined a gun club to learn how to handle firearms. She went to shooting competitions based on personal self defense scenarios. She took classes on food preservation such as canning and dehydrating foods. She started gardening and taught her children how to tend the gardens and harvest berries, tomatoes, and salad greens. Jake got on board with his wife's fervent interest and researched "bugging out" if a catastrophic event required them to leave their home in Florida. To him the worst case scenario was a nuclear bomb detonation anywhere in the Southeast. The Patriots story described families from Chicago moving to a farm in Northern Idaho. But he couldn't imagine moving from Florida to Idaho, nor could he find a place in the Southeast preferable over their home to go to. Except for the sea. Jake had always been a boater growing up. His family had multiple boats and lived near Tampa Bay in Florida. Jake borrowed against his retirement savings to purchase a twenty-year-old 45 foot cabin cruiser. It needed a lot of work. And he spent his spare time rebuilding the twin diesel engines, updating the electrical and plumbing systems, and cleaning up the berths and decks. He used every available inch of space for storage of food and medical supplies, too. He purchased a state-of-the-art weather station, GPS and navigation systems, radar, and defensive components, because piracy on the high seas was a growing problem worldwide. Jake also researched islands that were uninhabited in the Bahamas and the West Indies. He researched the governments of those islands to find which would favor mooring a yacht like his. He made sure the kids each had passports, good for the next 10 years. And he exchanged U.S. dollars for Bahamian dollars, Eastern Caribbean dollars used in Antigua and Barbuda and other island nations, Euros for use in Martinique, Dominican pesos for use in the Dominican Republic, Aruban florin for use in Aruba, plus a few others. His boat was ready and the family took weekend trips on it once per month to practice "bugging out", using the boat, and practicing navigation. Plus they had enjoyable family time exploring the Floridian waterways. Their plan was to live aboard, roaming the islands, until it was safe to return, if they ever had to leave their home in Florida.

As soon as Mari was ready, they would leave for the Islands. They would take his in-laws as they discussed and offer to take Jasmine, if she would go, too.

The phone buzzed in his pocket. He pulled away from Jasmine and saw that Congressman Ray Blanzing was calling him back. "Ray! Thanks for calling."

"Hi J.B. When will you be back to your office?"

J.B. knew something was up. "I'm on my way there now. Should be about 15 minutes. Do you want me to stop by your office on my way in?"

"Yeah, do that."

"I have someone with me. Do we need to be secure?"

"Who is it or can you not say?"

"I don't know if you saw me on ECF News this morning. But I was briefly kidnapped along with another person that was on ECF on the same story. We had to go to the hospital afterwards. She's from out of town. Since we were worried this kind of thing could happen again, I offered to drive her with me today until she flies back to Florida tonight."

"Oh. I see. Well, bring her by. She can wait in the anteroom while we get caught up."

"Sure. I'll see you in a few."

Jasmine reflected on the side of the conversation she could hear. She was liking this man more and more, even though he was being protective, or maybe because of it. Just then, her phone buzzed in her pocket. "Yes?"

It was Mari. "Hi Jazz."

"Mari, oh, how are you sis?"

"I'm off the pain medicines and I'm healing well. I'm ready to get out of here and see my kids."

"Oh, I bet."

"Where are you now?"

"Well." Jasmine looked over at J.B. as he smiled gently at her. "I'm in a chauffeured car with a Congressman!"

Mari did a double take, "What?"

"Yes, we were both interviewed on the same news story by ECF last night and this morning. I decided to stay here for the rest of today and will fly back tonight."

"Oh really?" Mari asked with a hint of suspicion at the glee in Jasmine's voice. "Didn't you have a rough couple of days, too?"

"Yes, I did. But I'm okay now. Just like you."

"Well, good. Look, Jazz, Jake and I are going to execute Plan B. Do you remember what that is?"

Jasmine stared for a moment out the front window. She replayed Mari's voice in her head again and processed this, focusing on listening. "Yes."

"Are you coming with us? Our ETD is tomorrow at high noon. From the *Point of Departure*."

Jasmine had been on their boat several times and knew the drill, though she had assured herself that *Point of Departure* was merely a pleasure boat and the point was to have family fun in the sun.

"I don't think I can make it in time. But I can rendezvous with you later."

"Ok. If we miss you, go to Point A, then B, and so on until you catch us. Do you remember the sequence?"

Jasmine had cryptic notes in her iPad. "Yes, I can catch you."

"Love you girl."

"Love you too, sis." And they hung up. Jasmine had to think about this. In one short weekend her world was unraveling. It was just two days ago she was paddling her kayak on the Indian River enjoying the sunset, and focusing on her latest sales pitches at work. Since then her sister had been stabbed, the kids' had three different caregivers, her parents had to leave their retirement, she had been assaulted by the TSA, and kidnapped by goons, and met this kind gentleman who taught her to defend herself with lethal force. And now they were ready to depart the world she knew well because of a sense the world was about to change dramatically. What a couple of days. She just realized she had to call her boss to tell him she might be delayed another day...

ELEVEN
Monday Afternoon, Rayburn House Office Building

The car arrived in an underground parking garage near the Capitol. They stepped out and headed for the elevator door. J.B. was explaining that Ray Blanzing had been his mentor when he started on Capitol Hill a few years before and they had since worked closely on coalitions, legislation, policy, and information exchange. Ray had been there a long time and understood all the nuances of the town. J.B. thought of him like a father-figure.

The elevator brought them to the 4th floor of the Rayburn House Office Building. The halls were large, clean, and formal. The terrazzo floor glistened as their footsteps clicked along with them. They walked to the end of the current hall to a door near the end. It had a simple sign "Congressman Ray Blanzing". They stepped through the carved mahogany door onto new lavender and sage-green carpeting that was soothing and restful. An immaculate assistant sat at a carved wood desk at the opposite end of the room and greeted them simply "Congressman. Ma'am".

J.B. replied," Hi Ranee." (It sounded just like "rainy".) J.B. pointed to a leather sofa on the side wall for Jasmine to sit down. She did and grabbed *The American Spectator* magazine from the coffee table in front of her. J.B. sat next to her and pulled out his phone to check for messages, tweets, and headlines. Within 5 minutes a man with a commanding appearance stepped through the door. His hair was a salted mix of a light shade of mouse-gray. Though it was thin and soft, it covered his head. Though he was of medium-height, he had "the look". The look of a former military man: erect posture, rugged lines about the face, and confidence. Congressman Ray Blanzing was in charge of his destiny. He stepped out of the inner office and glided over to greet them. J.B. stood up and shook the man's hand. As he leaned over to shake Jasmine's hand, she noticed his face was more wrinkled with age than his commanding appearance revealed. He announced to her, "Ray Blanzing".

"It is an honor to meet you, sir; Jasmine Roberts."

"I hear you have had two major ordeals while traveling through our Great Republic, one at the groping hands of our government and another by the terrifying hands of criminals."

"You put it so succinctly. But yes, I have."

"On behalf of the United States of America, I apologize for the former's overzealous nature and I condemn them both for violating your unalienable rights."

"I appreciate that," was all she could manage in light of the strength and provocative nature of his words.

"Please excuse us." She sat back down to read about the recent policies of the Federal Reserve.

The view was spectacular. He soaked it all in. He didn't ponder the past much but always enjoyed the present. He reminded himself every day of his wealth; he had plotted his net worth on graph paper ever since he was 18 years old. Now he kept an electronic board in his office with all his personal wealth statistics and graphs at the ready. As his assets were bought and sold in worldwide markets by his staff of 20 of the top financiers on the 20th floor of his multi-story complex just east of Manhattan's Battery City and southwest of Ground Zero, he reflected on his success. Though his net worth had hit one billion dollars several years ago, he was nearing 10 billion. He compared his goal chart with his actual chart and found he continued to exceed his goals, increasing his net worth tenfold every 6-7 years. He checked another wall-mounted monitor that included an executive information system dashboard, tracking dozens of news outlets in the U.S. and around the world. Frequencies of key words were shown by relative font sizes in the one quadrant of the display, along with world-wide market tickers in another quadrant, and natural events in a third quadrant. Such natural events included out of the ordinary weather, volcanoes, earthquakes, and so forth. Volcanoes erupt on the Earth's surface every single day. But most of them are remote enough that no one cares. However, when a volcano affects human production and livelihoods, then it affects world-wide macroeconomics. Earthquakes also occur every day somewhere in the world, with an amazing frequency. But most of them are either small enough or occur in lightly inhabited places that no one cares. But when they happen in Haiti, as they did in late 2009, people die, lose their homes, and lose their livelihoods. That is when Star's various industrial and transportation companies shift their resource distribution contracts to the highest bidder, setting the prices higher citing the increased demand from an earthquake in Haiti, a volcano in Iceland, or a tsunami in Japan.

Star enjoyed his view, enjoyed his empire. He had been pulling his minions along the ride for their utopian dreams of using *government* as their means of overseeing everything. Once a few people control everything then all the world's problems will be solved. And he would be one of the people controlling everything, naturally. He had believed in this dream most of his life. But lately he wondered how much different the world would become when the job is done. He had been making improvements to society his whole life and it seemed to no avail. Poverty was still a problem. Joblessness. Vices were still widely employed by the masses. Free thinkers still resisted and could not be convinced. Star was getting tired of the game. He was seeking new excitement but wasn't sure where to look, what it could be. He didn't have anyone that understood his need for new conquests.

Ah, but next week was time for his quarterly meeting with Rockefeller Warton. Rocky, his old nemesis, could not be allowed to win the battle. Star was confident his side was winning and he'd finally put Rocky in his place.

Their game had begun in 1980 when they both were attending Princeton and were in the Whig-Clio debating club. Reagan and Carter were campaigning for the Presidency and the debating club wanted to explore the same themes. It was Star v Warton and hundreds of people attended. They sparred on macroeconomics. They sparred on the nature of the threats to America worldwide. They dueled in words on all sorts of current issues, historical themes, and future paths to brighter times to come.

Warton had won the girl, Star won the debate. Warton won the election, Star won the first million dollars, though Warton won the race for the first $10 million. They had competed ever since in all ways. They met every quarter to see who was in the lead in each area of competition. Their deadline was fast approaching for the final prize. Star had bet the U.S. would become a European social democracy while Rocky had bet the U.S. would revert back to a federal republic. Star acknowledged he was in the lead given the progress of the 20th century: compulsion schooling that dumbs down the masses, entitlement retirement and health care programs that enslave the masses, Federal oversight on every aspect of commerce neutering the States and the federal system, and massive regulation preventing individuals from choosing their own livelihoods, thus leaving governments in charge of how many plumbers, doctors, teachers and scientists there are, deciding for people what their lot in life will be.

Star had lectured Warton in defense of social democracies that generally the people are too busy pursuing their happiness: raising families, improving their careers, and following their sports, hobbies, and interests to have time to be engaged in policy-making. Governance and policy had to be the responsibility of *some* of the people and not *all* of the people. After all, he argued, that's why we have representatives serving as policy makers: their job is to pay attention to the issues and create or modify laws that adapt to new technologies, new conditions, new threats around the world, the changing times. The regular people didn't want that responsibility; otherwise there would be a *true* democracy where *all* the people would vote on *all* the issues. Because the people are unaware of most of the aspects of each issue, they choose intelligent, educated, and informed people to run governments. Those people know better than the ones glued to March Madness playoffs or their PTA-coffee-klatches. The Europeans had already solved this problem by setting up their central governments with proportionate representation of the various concerns and building coalitions to manage resources, trade agreements, and balancing the needs of the various factions. Last, Star was able to show Warton a graph of the movement of power away from the States to the central government, *since the beginning of the Republic.* Thus, he felt confident he'd win the bet because of *momentum.* Star knew his only weakness would be a re-awakening of the people with characters similar to the Founders. That was his only concern. He had not been able to convince everyone. And he wasn't able to hypnotize the rest.

They had agreed then that for Star to win the wager, two indicators would prove him a winner by the end of 2014, 35 years after they started: first a single payer national health care system would exist and second, the national media would be under the control of the government. For Rocky to win, the Federal government's budget would be less than 18% of GDP for any year between 2000 and 2014 or the Federal debt would be reduced, or States would gain power, such as through an amendment, thus reversing the loss of States' rights ever since the Civil War and the 16th, 17th, and 21st amendments were passed. They decided that if neither side won by this time, they'd call it even. But if Star won, he'd pay Rocky $10,000 while if Rocky won, he'd pay Star $1,000, as they predicted in 1980 that Star had a 10 times greater chance of winning the bet than Rocky. Several members of their debating club witnessed the agreement when they made the bet the night of the debate, where they celebrated their freedom during a wild stag party of heavy drinking, drugs, co-eds, and other self-destructive behavior.

Ever since that bet, Star had been using all his growing power and influence to cause the socialist system he had wagered for. He never won the girl, he never won the friends, but he won the big things, the ones that counted. He refused to feel jealous that Rocky got the friends and the ladies in college, and now had a large close-knit family.

Back to the moment, he would call Kale again and push him harder. He had done well with the best friend bit but Bo had botched the job with the sister. It was time to take more steps.

The orderly wheeled Mari to the hospital entrance. She had bags of pills and instructions on her lap. Another orderly walked beside her with a cart full of flower bouquets, her overnight bag, her handbag, and a plastic bag of her clothes. Her rich brown hair was still damp following the shower she took an hour ago, upon news she would be released. Jake was by the rental car under the portico outside the door. He waved and the two orderlies brought Mari and her gear to the car. Jake helped Mari into the front seat and then stowed her things in the trunk. He said thank you to both the orderlies and waved good-bye as he stepped into the driver's side.

"We can be home in 8 hours. I have a full tank of gas and $500 in cash if we need anything. I have a cooler full of water and orange juice bottles and a bag full of cereals, breads, apples, and bananas. We can stop how often you want and get whatever you need. But if I don't hear from you, I'm going to try to drive straight through, okay?"

She nodded her head. She reclined her seat part way, put her head on Jake's jacket as a pillow and closed her eyes. She knew that rest was the single best thing she could do to be back on her feet as soon as possible. So she closed her eyes and made lists in her head of last minute details they might need to check. She had drilled bugging out so many weekend trips that she was able to rest her mind and fell asleep within minutes. Jake focused on the road and listened to talk radio to hear the reassuring sounds of nothing much important for the afternoon's news. He looked at his watch and saw they would beat the rush hour traffic of Atlanta by leaving now rather than later. He smiled with confidence that all their efforts would only help them go through the coming storms.

Rebecca keyed in the message on the communicator. If the President was available he could acknowledge the message when he was ready. In the old days, she would have "buzzed" him but President Clinton did not like being buzzed when he was working on a big issue because it interrupted his train of thought. So Motorola developed a different communicator system. Rebecca typed a message into her device. Inside the Oval office the device would remain silent if there was any sound in the room or any movement in the room. It would also stay silent if the President was sitting at the Resolute desk. Because if he were there, he could see the message on the display. If he was not there, he would only see from across the room that there was a message. Different low-glowing indicator lights would show the importance that Rebecca assigned to each message. It would glow red for a critical message and blue for a low-priority message. If there were both types of messages at once, it would glow purple. If there were a message of medium importance, and one of low importance, it would glow green, showing a combination of both yellow and blue message types. The color shade changed with the proportion of messages. And if there were several messages of all three types, the three primary colors merged to a shade of reddish-brown. Now if the President was not at his desk and wasn't speaking with someone in the room, it made a short audible sound. The pitch of the sound corresponded to the criticality of the most-critical of messages waiting – higher pitch sounds for more critical messages. If the President waved his arm, the audible sound would cease. If he didn't, it would repeat every 5 seconds until an arm wave or there was an audible sound.

He had finished the awards ceremonies at 3:30 pm. Now, a short time later, between signing folios, he reviewed the remarks he would say at 7:00 pm this evening on live TV about increasing security for the traveling public.

At the moment Orinthbey was sitting at his desk signing various forms and orders. He had the TV on across the room but was not watching; he was listening however, so the Comm did not make a sound. It did, however, flash a blue light and indicate a low priority message. Percival finished signing the last of the folios, closed and stacked them on a corner of the desk, and pressed the Comm button for Rebecca to come inside his office.

She was there an instant later, quietly sliding in from the door. "Yes, Mr. President?"

"I've finished these," he replied and handed her a stack of folios.

"Of course," she said waiting.

"So who's out there? I didn't look."

"It's Kale Evans. I know he doesn't have an appointment but he asked if you had a moment for him. He was here meeting with Mr. Roullin this afternoon." Roullin was the White House meeting coordinator.

"Well, I have a few minutes. Give me his low-down again."

Rebecca handed him a blue folio. He opened it and saw a profile of Mr. Kale Evans. It showed him that Evans had contributed $10,000 to his various campaigns over the years; that he was employed by the Brain as a coordinator of special functions, which he had visited the White House 15 times over the past 6 months. It showed him as single, never-married, long time resident of a wealthy neighborhood in D.C., and educated at the University of Chicago in sociology.

"How many times have I met him?"

Rebecca leaned over his desk and turned the page inside the folio. It said the two had met twice: once at a fundraiser for his campaign when Mr. Evans was there with Mr. Star and another time at a White House black tie dinner shortly after the inauguration.

"So what does he want?"

She shook her head slightly. "He doesn't want to tell me. If he did, he would have just left a message. What he did say is there on the bottom," she pointed at the page, "he said you both have a mutual problem and he has a proposed solution."

"I'll buzz you in about 3 minutes to let him in," as he waved her off.

Rebecca turned and efficiently exited the room and brought the folios with her. She set them on the inside corner of her desk and pressed several buttons on her console. These buttons let the offices of the people that needed the folios back to know to come to her desk and retrieve them. She glanced at her watch and pressed her timer button. POTUS always made people wait at least 3 minutes longer. She knew he was in there watching his console. He had a live video feed of the reception area so he could study his visitors as they waited for him. She also knew he would take the time to memorize the details of the folio report she had given him, so that he could warmly welcome his visitor with a personalized touch.

Orinthbey pressed the button early. It occurred to him that he could finish his day early the rate things were going. He might as well finish this visitor's inquiry to go get his dinner and relax for a time.

The door opened and Rebecca walked in, followed by Kale. She announced, "Mr. Kale Evans."

He did not look at his guest. Instead he looked at Rebecca and asked, "And, when do the media teams need to come in the evening for the video feed?"

"As soon as you are done with Mr. Evans they can set up their equipment."

"Thank you, Rebecca." She turned and left the room.

"Kale, so nice to see you. Thanks for coming by."

"Mr. President."

"Would you like a cold drink? A soda or a sparkling water?"

"No, thank you, sir."

Motioning to the sofa, "Well, please have a seat."

Kale sat down, feeling more nervous than he wanted.

"I haven't seen you in a long time, what was it…? The Bergoni dinner here at the White House?"

"Yes, that's right." Kale felt himself relaxing and getting over the jitters. But he still didn't know what small talk to make with the President.

"Well, what brings you by?" Orinthbey was sipping a frappucino through a straw and sat back comfortably in the sofa across and away from Kale.

"Sir, I have a proposal. I know that my employer, Mr. Star, often makes suggestions to you on policies that represent his sector of the business community."

"Mr. Star, hmmm…, yes on a few occasions we've talked, as I do with numerous influential people." Orinthbey was not comfortable divulging anything to anyone about his relationship with Star.

Kale swallowed hard on this, "Of course. Well, there have been times where I have tried to show Mr. Star better ways of solving the problems that are most important to him as he has stated them to me. Most times he and I agree and we proceed with our positions but there have been times when he resists my suggestions. This is a time when I think his resistance is a serious mistake. I think his goals can be realized by following my current suggestion."

Orinthbey leaned forward slightly, "Really? Go on."

"Look. I want to bring the mission to the next level. I'm ready now. And I know how to do it. Star isn't ready. He wants to continue with the incremental approach. For example, he thinks this stabbing on the airplane is an opportunity to prevent people from flying or traveling on public modes of transportation if they are mentally unstable. This will help people feel safer while traveling. Et cetera."

Orinthbey knew this was the case. He also remembered vividly the ache in the pit of his stomach he felt upon hearing how different Star's outlook on the issue was from his own. "I *think* I know what you are referring to. I thought the incident on the plane was a cause to make the public feel that our methods are working well and that a disaster was averted. Praises to the institution of Homeland Security."

Kale pondered what he had just heard. Clearly Star didn't have complete control of this President, even though he claimed 110% loyalty. This President hadn't asserted himself, he just needed a reason to feel comfortable doing so. "Do you know what my job is in Star Enterprises?"

Orinthbey thought back to his folio. He saw the image of the page in his mind's eye, given that he had a photographic memory. He saw the words printed on the page, "special functions coordinator". He leaned farther forward toward Kale, "No, enlighten me."

"I'm the one that provides Star access to hundreds of community groups, associations, and organizations. I meet with the leaders of those groups regularly. I advise the leaders on how to keep their members active: funding, responsive, and agreeable. They have plenty of control of their legions. And I control them. I advise them how to appease members that threaten their leadership status. And I have those second tier people under my control, too. This is all I do. This is my entire career. And I'm really good at it. Do you remember the *Cleaners Cause?* That was a world-wide strike of a million people that I orchestrated. I also orchestrated the *Mechanics Message* strike and the *Justice for All* march on Washington a few years back.

"Did you arrange the Air Traffic Controllers strike in the 1980s?"

"Yes. We exerted our power even though the outcome was unforeseen. Look. I have their loyalties. I pull all the strings on hundreds of thousands of people ready to do our bidding whenever we need them. Star depends on me entirely to bring out the people en masse to support his objectives *around the world*. We've done it many times over the past 30 or so years. I know these people and I know they are ready *today* for the tidal wave to sweep over this land. They don't want any more ripples that sweep small bits of the beach away. They want the tidal wave to transform us finally to a nation where working people are *equal* in all ways."

Quite the speech, thought Orinthbey. So this was the man that Star protected. Star didn't brag very often. He was tight-lipped. But there were a couple of times when he talked about the stops he could pull by the size of the army he had ready for revolution. "That sounds like a lot of influence. How did you amass so much power?"

"Let's just say I *know* people. I know what their buttons are and how to push them. I know what they need to hear. Star's an idiot. He thinks he can just boss people into submission. He does it to me every day. I take his diatribes because I need his money to complete my mission. He gives me whatever budget I need and I deliver the results – I get the people out to support our goals using his money. It works. We pay for buses to bring people in. We compile email lists and mail out newsletters. We have offices in every poor neighborhood of large enough numbers of people. And we have one more thing. We are *prepared*."

"Prepared? Prepared for what?"

"Well, Mr. President, in order to get armies of poor people to revolt in the street, you have to ensure they can be out there for days and weeks if needbe. You have to *sustain* them. In other words, you have to get them food and water. We are prepared to feed hundreds of thousands of people for weeks when they come out and protest and demand change. We are prepared to fight the battles that need to be fought to make the tidal wave sweep over the nation and end the greed of capitalism forever."

Orinthbey wasn't too comfortable with this part of the conversation. He realized that if enough people revolted it would reflect badly on his Presidency. He also knew they could demand his resignation, *or worse*. He didn't know Star was building an army, *on purpose*, to overthrow the capitalist system. He wondered now what else he was missing, how he didn't see this, and he felt his head spin a bit from the feeling of falling, which jars one awake suddenly. He was being used far more than he had agreed to. He had only agreed to put Star's priorities high on the list and to meet with him regularly in exchange for Star's buying the Presidency for him – the election was bought and paid for by Star. This must have been the same army Star referred to get out the vote. Now with this ill feeling, he had to wonder what Kale was all about. "So, what exactly are you proposing?"

"A partnership. You and me."

"Elaborate, please."

"Well, I deliver this army to you, we tip the balance of power, and you and I run the utopian society on the other side."

"That sounds simple enough. What is involved in 'tipping the balance of power'?" At this point, Percival reached his hand under the sofa cushion and slid his fingertip across a small thin metal trinket that looked like a coin. It was a fingerprint sensor that recognized his fingerprints and started recording everything in the room.

"I propose, Mr. President, that I order my armies to get out into the streets to protest the failures of the airlines in preventing stabbings on airplanes. We will blame the airlines. We will blame the oil companies for squeezing the airlines. Both of these are due to corporate greed and Wall Street. We will demand more funding for mental health counseling to keep dangerous people locked up, like the people on that flight. We will demand more government funding of transportation. We will demand a government takeover of the airlines so that everyone can travel, even the poorest people. And the government will decide who gets to fly and who doesn't *for our own safety*.

"We'll cause chaos for travelers. We will then spread that chaos to shipping, trucking, and busing affecting daily life. We'll topple the transportation infrastructure that allows capitalism to work. Once we control transportation the rest will fall in place. You will sweep in and take over the airlines and the trucking industry and restore order but you will have rule by decree to do this. And once you fix the problems with the transportation and distribution system you have everything."

Orinthbey was wondering what he had gotten himself into. He thought Star was interested in a European style social democracy like himself, a socialist. Now, this guy, Kale, doing most of Star's work, was an anarchist. Or a communist. Or just a radical power-monger. Deciding to keep the charade going he asked, "So what would your role be in this grand scheme?"

"You'll be promoted to Prime Minister and I'll be President. Your role will be to run Defense, State, and National Security. My role will be to run domestic programs like Health, Housing, and Commerce."

Knowing he was recording this he said, "I see…. Kale, I find all this a bit hard to believe. Do you disagree that the progress we've made over the past 100 years hasn't been good and worth it?"

"Of course it's been good and worth it."

"We've come so far. We control all commerce, all banking, and **all** the money supply. We control education so the young buy-in to our world view. We're almost finished with single payer health care with only five health insurance companies left standing. We control the food supply. All we have left are communications and guns."

"And transportation. That's why you need my army – to disarm the people once the protests and potential riots begin."

"Do you think you can control the outcome of what you're proposing?"

"Sure I do, I have the loyalties of all the leaders and second and third tier people in those groups."

"What about the loyalties of the flash mobs?" Flash mobs were dozens of small troops of young people that suddenly and unexpectedly went out of control, robbing shops, knocking over people, committing assaults, vandalism, and other quick, unplanned crimes. "What about the loyalties of the people that get frenzied up by your protests and commit major crimes? What about the anarchists that show up at these things and want to take things to the next level? How do you control *them*? How do you prevent blood in the streets?"

"I'm not worried about blood in the streets. Didn't you ever learn about the French Revolution?"

119

"The French Revolution was <u>not</u> a good thing."

Just then Kale realized that Orinthbey was not on the same team. This wasn't *his* dream. Was this why Star wasn't pushing harder? Was this why Star was still taking small, incremental steps? He felt like he needed to get away quickly, that coming here was all a mistake. "I guess I've taken enough of your time and should be going," he said as he stood up to leave.

Orinthbey made no move to leave. "Sit down, Kale."

Kale sat back down.

"I want change just as much as you and Star do. We're making that change. We're making progress every day. But I cannot be a party to blood on the streets. No President can. We take an oath of office. We want what's best for <u>all</u> the people. While I want to be on the other side of this mess, too, in our utopian society, we will get there. We already have the power to control transportation and the military. The military is *obligated* to follow my orders. Next is communications. I'm pushing for government news feeds to replace AP and Reuters. I'm pushing for government control of the backbone of the Internet in order to protect the Internet from cyber attacks. I'll be able to shut it down with the push of one button! We already have access to text messages, emails, cell phone locations, and the GPS systems of newer automobiles. This means we know where everyone is, what they're saying, and whom they're saying it to. Already. Once the government news feeds are in place, we'll have the leverage to take over the *New York Times,* the *LA Times* and the *Washington Post.* That will be easy with their diving circulation rates. We just weaken them, bail them out, and then take them over. I'm limiting issuance of broadcast licenses. I'm encouraging our wealthy allies to buy up all the news organizations they can. We're almost there. We have much of transportation already, too. We control fuel taxes. We regulate the trucking industry. A couple of major wrecks and we'll be able to restrict trucking even more. One bad train wreck and we'll be able to limit freight transport, too.

"I want you to help me solve the communications piece. I want you to use your resources and your smarts to quiet the opposition long enough to pull the remaining strings. Hang in there, Kale, and thanks for stopping by". He said this as he rose to say goodbye. Kale stood back up and Orinthbey reached out to shake his hand. After a brief handshake, Kale turned to leave.

Orinthbey followed him out and waved good-bye. As soon as Kale was gone down the hall and out of earshot, Orinthbey turned to Rebecca and said, "Assemble the A team in the Situation room at once. And don't let that man back in the White House again.

Percival went back into the Oval office and slurped his melting frappucino. He had made a stand. The first one of his Presidency. He hoped it was the right stand.

TWELVE

Monday Afternoon, Situation Room, White House

They rose from their chairs to stand as President Orinthbey entered the room. The A team consisted of the Secretary of Defense, the Secretary of State, the Secretary of Homeland Security and the National Security Advisor. They were silent until he spoke as they wondered what he could know first, that none of them were yet aware. "Please sit down," he announced as he sat at the head of the table in the small, high-tech room. "A fellow that apparently meets regularly with our own Roullin just stopped in to see me. It seems he has or at least thinks he has a lot of pull to mobilize hundreds of thousands of people to protest in the streets, perhaps even violently. Now, he didn't make demands of me in exchange to avoid such protests but he did encourage policy decisions on my part to make *use* of such protests. I discouraged him, sent him away, and blocked his access to return to the White House. What I need from you are three questions answered. First, is he as powerful as he says he is? Second, will he move ahead with mobilizing his army regardless of what we do, and third, what steps can we take to both stop him and stop the people that are following him?"

Bella had opened the line on her phone to her deputy at the CIA before she arrived in this meeting. Her trusted colleague there was listening and taking action while the President spoke. She had anticipated this some time ago, when she was still at the CIA. But she didn't know how such power might manifest itself. Now she had a lead.

"Dismissed," announced the President. After they filed out Orinthbey thought about how hungry he was. He stayed in his chair alone in the Situation room. He called the Chef and made a request for his dinner for steak, a loaded baked potato, and a Caesar salad. He had an hour or so to go, so he returned to his office and practiced his speech for tonight as the news feed team set up.

She watched him emerge from the side door. She positioned her car to the sidewalk to intercept him. Ritalia waited as he made the long walk. She checked her appearance in the rear-view mirror: large, dark eyes, smooth deep complexion, and long, wavy black hair glistening in the late daylight. Kale opened the passenger door and climbed in. Now that her boss was retrieved, she asked, "How did it go?"

"Not good. He's not interested! Star makes it sound like he's completely onboard and completely in Star's control. Either Star is wrong or he's been lying to me," he shook his head in disgust with himself for entrusting Star so much with the plans. "I'll assemble the team as soon as we get back."

Twenty minutes later they entered the basement of his home. A gleaming array of controllers glowed in the air above the table and hummed their electronic wizardry while Kale pulled up a chair and moved his fingers across a series of lights in the space, connected by the sense of motion to his every command. In moments, the array displayed a sort of treasure map with highlighted icons glowing to indicate a live connection or not. Kale spoke one word, "Roll," and each icon took a turn growing large, with a corresponding synthesized voice proclaiming "Here," each in turn. Once the roll call was complete, Kale said, "The rabbit won't hop. We can proceed on our own or we can wait longer. Vote 'aye' to proceed and 'nay' to wait. Kale listened as the vote was taken. It took several minutes. There were 45 of these leaders on this call. They could not hear each other but they knew they were all connected, through their leader, Kale Evans. They didn't know how the others were voting. They had to trust Kale's account of the vote. When the ayes and nays were counted, Kale announced the result. "The vote is split. 24 for and 21 against." Just then one icon spoke to Kale and suggested that the bunny's successor would be more conducive. Maybe this was the time for the Negative 1 plan. Kale announced, "Because we are split, let's vote on the Negative 1 plan, which one of us has recommended". Kale counted the ayes and nays again. He was surprised at the outcome, "The ayes have it clearly, with 38 for and 7 against. Any discussion?" he waited, before opening the channel for everyone to hear everyone else. There was none. "Ok. Plan Negative 1 will commence shortly."

Because Kale didn't do messy work, he waited until everyone disconnected. The leader that suggested this plan remained on the line and said in his deep and gritty synthesized voice that he would handle the event. Kale asked when he should contact Number 2 and the voice said, "Not until Number 2 is installed".

The days' events were catching up with Jasmine. The longer she sat here waiting for J.B., the more restless she became. She was wondering why she was sitting here. Her mother taught her long ago that if she ever asked that

124

question of herself, it meant she probably shouldn't be wherever she was at the time. It had been nearly an hour and she realized she should be thinking about how to get back home and get back to work.

She picked up her magazine and tried to read the article again. It was a summary of how the Federal Reserve was founded at a place called Jekyll Island in near-complete secrecy, what its objectives were, and how it was managed. For example, the President does not choose the members of the Board of Governors and the Chairman. Instead the Board provides a short list of candidates from which the President can nominate. In other words, it's an exclusive insiders club. She read that their portfolio was enormous and she wondered how they could possibly have such a staggering array of assets. She pulled out her wallet and looked at the currency she had with her. The twenty, the five, the ten dollar bills all said "Federal Reserve Note" and she realized that the entire monetary system, which was entirely based on *faith*, did not belong to the People but belonged to this exclusive club of Governors that no one could penetrate without an invitation from its members. Her unease doubled. And she felt more exhausted than ever.

ECF News ran the news first. The ticker moved across the screen: "WHITE HOUSE MEDICAL TEAM MUSTERED BECAUSE OF AN EMERGENCY – UPDATE PENDING". The producer chose not to hand this story to the anchor until more details came in. Jasmine had looked up at that moment and wondered what that could mean. She looked out the window of the office building they were in and saw dozens of police cars blocking Maryland Avenue, Independence Avenue, and the surrounding streets. Then she saw several fire trucks of all sizes move past the Capitol toward the White House. She quickly put two and two together that the activity outside the window was related to the ticker. She pulled out her cell phone and called Namia Pruvati. Namia answered, "Namia Pruvati."

"Hi Namia, this is Jasmine Roberts. I just saw the ticker on ECF about the White House medical team and I wanted to let you know I'm in the Rayburn House office building at the moment and I can see dozens of police and fire truck vehicles between here and there."

"How many police cars in your view and what are they doing?"

Jasmine counted them, "Fourteen police cars from my viewpoint. They are blocking all traffic from entering Independence Avenue, Maryland Avenue, and from my vantage point Pennsylvania Avenue, too and all surrounding streets."

"Interesting. How many fire trucks? Or are they EMTs?"

"I don't know the difference between EMT and fire trucks. They are all painted-red and have flashing lights on and are various sizes."

"Okay. How many and what are they doing?"

Jasmine counted these. "I see fifteen trucks, 5 of them large, like ladder trucks, and the other ten are mid-size. A few of them are moving slowly toward the White House and the rest look like they are stuck or parked."

"Thanks soooo much, Jasmine. Please don't hesitate to call me if you learn anything more. I am going to hang up now, though, to take a few more calls. Also, where are you and why are you there?"

"Like I said I'm in the Rayburn Building. After leaving ECF this morning, the other interviewee, J.B. Stanton, offered to drive me to the airport in his car. My flight isn't until tonight so I'm on Capitol Hill with him while he is doing the People's business until my flight."

"Ok. I don't need to include that but it helps me."

She continued to watch the TV while also glancing out the windows. She pulled out a piece of paper and wrote her notes down of the time of day, the number of police cars, and fire trucks. She made notes of what they were doing. She also walked over to the TV and turned up the volume. A few minutes later Blanzing and Stanton came out of Blanzing's office. J.B. saw the look of alarm on Jasmine's face, "What is it?"

"Look out the window at all the emergency vehicles! And ECF just reported on its ticker that the White House medical team has been mustered. But that's all I know so far."

Blanzing went back into his office and picked up his desk phone and made a call. Just then, Namia Pruvati was introduced by the anchor as she was in a separate studio to report. "We have word that the President may be injured inside the White House; that the medical team has been mustered to provide medical care; and that dozens of police cars and fire trucks are deployed for several blocks surrounding the White House. It's unclear at this time whether they are there to escort the injured persons to the hospital or to provide a roadblock to prevent parties of interest from leaving the area around the White House. We'll bring you more as we learn it. This is Namia Pruvati, reporting from the Nation's Capital."

Stanton stepped out of his office. He leaned in toward J.B. and murmured, "The President is ill. Very sick. Sudden onset."

"What does that *mean*?"

"It seems they are investigating the possibility of a deliberate poisoning."

"Oh, crap."

"And I think you both may be stuck here. The police have not only blocked off the western access of the Capitol but all surrounding streets. That is, none of us can leave."

Jasmine looked at her watch. It was after 5:00 pm. She was planning to head to the airport by 6:30 for her 8:00 pm flight. She looked out the window again and it hit her that she was unlikely to make her flight this evening. She texted her boss with an update, "Stuck in Capitol; DC Shutdown. More later."

* * * * *

The Vice President was jogging on a treadmill in the room adjacent to her office at Number One Observatory Circle when her Chief of Staff stepped in. He handed her a slip of paper that was yellow. This was a signal that the message was urgent. She put it on top of her book on the control panel of the treadmill and read the news that the President was ill and she may have to step in temporarily. She looked up at Ricardo.

"Tell me everything," as she climbed off the treadmill and walked into her bathroom and turned on the shower.

"Rebecca called me 3 minutes ago with the news that Orinthbey went down to see the chef for a solo dinner after he practiced his speech for this evening. While he was eating he passed out on the table into his food. The chef was there with him and pressed the panic button. Every asset immediately responded: police, EMT, fire, and descended on the White House. When Rebecca saw the alert, she went to see the President but he was unconscious. So she called me. And I'm telling you."

By this time, Vice President Alice Bergurner had stripped completely naked in front of her Chief of Staff, without an ounce of modesty, and entered the steaming hot shower. Ricardo was accustomed to knowing all of the most intimate details about the VP because she kept nothing from him. Theirs was a complete partnership. "So no one has confirmed yet what ails the President, what his condition is, whether he has a directive for us?"

"No, we got the first call. Now, I've already called our driver to get the car ready and pick you up. I've asked Rebecca to assemble as many of the Staff and Secretaries as possible into the Situation room to coincide with your arrival, which I have estimated in 20 minutes from now."

"Excellent Ricardo."

"I have not alerted the Press to anything until we know more of the President's condition and how long it will be until he resumes his duties. However, he was supposed to give a live speech at 7:00 this evening, according to Rebecca."

Ricardo looked at his Smartphone and saw the ECF tweet that someone at the White House was ill and EMTs had surrounded the neighborhood. He looked up at Alice as she stepped out of the shower, her mature body still robust. He understood why she was so proud. "Didn't you say he practiced the speech? Is there a recording? Call Rebecca and see if she can run that. Have her tell the video feed team that the President has a situation in the Ivory Coast to address and won't be able to do the speech live."

"The Ivory Coast?"

"Yes, I'll call the Ambassador and ask him to release a statement to the Press which plausibly explains the crisis the President has to attend to so they won't be suspicious."

"Ok." He called Rebecca back with the plan about running the recording and the crisis with the Ivory Coast. He got the number for the Ambassador from Rebecca who was a walking encyclopedia. He turned around and Bergurner was dressed, had pinned up her wet hair, and slid into her suit jacket. She slipped on her pumps and they walked out the door, down the hall, and out the door to where the car was waiting. Ricardo dialed the number to the Ambassador and he answered as Bergurner stepped into the car. She proceeded with her request of the Ambassador while she put on her makeup and the car sailed swiftly down the city streets. As they arrived at a police roadblock, Ricardo spoke to the officer and explained who they were. They were allowed to pass. By this time, Alice was drying her hair in the back seat and pinning it back up into place. Ricardo also let Rebecca know they were arriving and the entry team let them in quickly and quietly.

THIRTEEN

Monday Evening, White House

"Get me everything you have. This has to be deliberate." Gliad hung up the phone as she walked briskly to the basement of the White House. She kept shaking her head in disbelief. Her phone rang again. It was Rebecca.

"Hi Rebecca."

"Madame Secretary, the Vice President is on her way to the White House."

"Thanks for letting me know. Have you assembled everyone?"

"I'm still working on it. Sit Room 20 minutes. Okay?"

"Yes, thank you."

Bella was allowed to watch the interrogation of the Chef by the Secret Service for a few minutes. When the 20 minutes was getting close, she eyed the Chief and nodded her head to the side. They spoke in hushed tones behind a structural column at the edge of the kitchen. "Alice is on her way. You need to double up protection of her. And monitoring."

He gave Gliad a sidelong stare.

"Look, Chief. Someone did this on purpose to Orinthbey. That someone couldn't get what they want from Perc and so they are going to pressure Alice to do their bidding instead. You have to make sure they don't have access, certainly no exclusive access, and no opportunity to affect her."

"Yes, Madame Secretary," he winked. And she gave a small chuckle at how he said her title. The Chief reported to her when she was in Intelligence. They were on the same page.

As the car approached the White House, the driver got a call on his communicator. He pressed the "ACK" button on his wrist. In his ear he heard the words, "Wrap up the package. 'A' level threat." The driver pressed the "ACK" button again and glanced in his rearview mirror. The 'package' didn't even know he got this call. She transformed herself from the shower to Madame V.P. in the time it took to deliver her.

Bella had not yet sat down in the Sit room when the door opened and the Vice President strode in after her. She greeted the VP as did the others, standing, until the venerable Alice Bergurner sat in the President's chair. Her chief joined her by standing behind her right side against the wall.

"Thank you all for coming. Please correct me if my understanding is incorrect. I have heard the President is ill and unconscious and that Rebecca summoned us all here for this meeting," she began.

Bella leaned forward, "We suspect this was a deliberate attack, not an accident or an illness."

"Really? On what basis?"

"The President was in excellent health as witnessed by several people immediately before going to supper. And the

Chef tasted all the items he served to the President before the President tasted them himself," Bella reported.

"Has anyone talked with the medical team yet?"

Rebecca walked in just then and spoke to the group, rather than giving a message to the Vice President. "The Chief of Staff is remaining with the President. He asked me to relay the latest information with you. The medical team is transporting the President to the hospital at this moment. He remains unconscious. Based on evidence at the scene of his collapse, the FBI is here investigating a possible poisoning.

"The President practiced his remarks for tonight's live broadcast and I know he wanted to give that speech. His remarks *are* recorded and could be used in the live time slot in lieu of an alternative.

"Here is what I need in order for the White House to function. I need to know from you (a) what you, as a group, decide to issue to the press and how. For example, if you want to hold a press conference, I need 30 minutes notice to arrange it. And (b) under Amendment 25, Section 4 of the U.S. Constitution, I have drafted a declaration to be transmitted to the President Pro Tempore and the Speaker to swear in Madame Bergurner as Acting President. For now, you are obligated to follow your continued directives until the President recovers unless a majority of you sign this and the President and Speaker accept it," she handed the folio with the declaration to Bella, and continued, "And (c) if at such time you decide to swear in the V.P., I need to know whether you plan to have the press present or not. The White House photography team has to be there, too." She glanced at her watch, "You have thirty minutes to deliberate before I need to hear the decisions. Also, if the Speaker arrives, I will send him in. And if any of the other Cabinet officers arrive, I will also send them in. Finally, if there are any updates to the President's condition, I will share that with you. If the President recovers before you complete the task set before you, then this meeting will immediately be nullified." And she turned and left without fielding a single question.

Both Alice and Bella began to speak at the same time. Then they both stopped together. Both waited for the other to yield but when neither did, they both started to speak again. At this point, the National Security Advisor, Ron Price spoke up, "In my opinion we should continue with our directives as long as possible and wait to convert the VP to Acting until we have run out of other options," he announced as though Alice was not in the room.

Alice gave him a long, hard look. As she was about to rebut, both she and Bella started to speak at the same moment for a third time. This time the Secretary of Defense spoke, "I agree with Ron. We should assume the President will be back to work within a couple of hours. However, I think you should stay here tonight, Alice, so we can swear you in at a moment's notice."

This time Bella did not hesitate, "I concur. At this point we have every reason to believe the President will be well enough to return to his duties at any moment. Until the medical team indicates that he will be incapacitated and tells us for how long we should assume he'll be back to work momentarily. I also think we should run the tape tonight in the time slot he would have done it live."

Alice spoke this time, "I agree with all three of you. In fact, I've already run interference by calling the ambassador to the Ivory Coast to report to us with the unrest there as the reason the President cannot deliver his remarks live tonight and we must resort to using the video. Additionally, I think the Press Secretary should release a written statement to the Press saying the President ate something that was disagreeable and was taken to the hospital as a precaution. We'll remind them of the time Bush 41 fainted during a State dinner overseas." She looked at the Defense Secretary and finished, "I will sleep here tonight, in the Lincoln Bedroom, so I can field all the calls and issues that come before the President until he resumes his duties. That is, I will be making the final call on any matters that come up until the President is returned from the hospital."

"No, I don't think so," replied Bella. If you read the directive," which she pulled from the folio in front of her, "in the event the President is temporarily inaccessible the Cabinet officers will administer their departments in full effect according to their last instructions and their own executive judgment. It does not say that we should ever consult with the Vice President. Until we need you to be sworn in as Acting President, we do not answer to you."

Alice was taken aback. She hadn't pressed to be sworn in now. She didn't vie for it. And yet she was being shut out at the very time her Country needed her. "But I am here to help! This is my job, to be the President's second-in-command. His backup. I believe it is appropriate for me to be the person that ensures his policies are followed."

This time Ron stepped in to respond, "We are sworn officers of the U.S. Constitution. We answer to the U.S. Congress. We know our roles and we know whom to consult whenever there is an issue too large for one of us. We also know your role under the Constitution, which is to preside over the Senate and to administer any functions the President has assigned to you. Let's see," he looked in one of the folders on the table, "to manage the Healthy Citizen program, to entertain dignitaries from the Southern Hemisphere, to attend public events as assigned by the Public Affairs Chief of the White House."

"Well and fine. I can live with that. I will be here ready when you decide you need me."

The French baguette bread was moist with the crust crumbly, the flavors of turkey, Swiss, mayonnaise and mustard, lettuce and tomato, all mixed together felt delicious in her mouth. She didn't realize how hungry she had been.

Across from her was J.B. and next to him was Ray Blanzing. They had gotten the word that they wouldn't be able to leave the building until at least 6:00 p.m. so they decided to eat in the sandwich bar. Though Ray had food in front of him, his phone was ringing constantly. He was in the loop and was getting news out of the White House. She and J.B. were enjoying their sandwiches and stealing looks at each other. When they were nearly done eating, Ray finally hung up his phone.

"The President is at the hospital now. They're pumping his stomach and monitoring his condition. Not sure how grave it is yet. Officially: he ate something *disagreeable*."

Suddenly Jasmine wished she hadn't eaten her whole sandwich, as her stomach lurched on that news. She looked at her watch, "Any chance I can still make it to the airport tonight?" As she asked she looked at J.B. and she was sure his expression became crestfallen.

"Let me find out," Ray responded and dialed his phone again while chewing another bite.

As he pressed the call button the alarms were sounded in the room and bright strobe lights blinked. The room went from quiet to a rush as everyone stood up from tables across the space at the same moment. Expressions went quickly from conversational to stunned. Jasmine, J.B., and Ray stood as well and exited the sandwich shop and headed toward the stairs. There, they joined a crowd doing the same.

As they neared the exit, the crowd thronged. It was a long, slow wait to get through the exit door, out into the cold evening. The sun was past the horizon and the sky's glow was dim. Jasmine felt the cold in her bones almost immediately. She knew that her stomach full of sandwich was part of the reason, as the human body's blood flow transfers from the muscles to the digestive tract after eating, thus there is less heat available in the arms and legs. Plus it was downright cold.

Ray had been on the phone the entire time they were heading for the exit, he led the three of them beyond the crowd milling outside the door, along the path under the trees and to the driveway, where his car was waiting. The three of them filed in, while Ray was still on the phone. He finally clicked off his call and explained, "There are dozens of bomb threats every day in the Nation's capital. The D.C. police have the most sophisticated tools available to assign likelihood ratings to each call, based on from where the call is placed, the caller's voice quality, and a myriad of sensors throughout the capital that measure quantities of trace chemical elements, being able to sniff out a Mr. Greenthumb lawn chemical treatment professional on vacation with his family visiting the Air & Space Museum by the chemical residue in his hair, under his fingernails, and caked into his shoes. So most all the calls are rated as false alarms or hoaxes. But because of what has happened to the President, they are treating every single call as real until they sort out how he could have been compromised."

Though they were comfortably settled into the car and the heat was on, the driver was not able to move the car far – cars were backed up in all directions around them. It seemed it would be a long time before they could leave the city. She called the airline to say she was stuck in D.C. traffic and might miss her flight. She called her boss to let him know the same. They she rested her head on J.B.'s shoulder and pondered the long day and all that she had learned about her Country. What she saw and what she knew of Mari's efforts to straighten the world out had her feeling hopeless at this moment. She wasn't quite asleep but not awake either as she lightly dreamed. Her dreams were filled with playful times at the beach interrupted by TSA-uniform-wearing thugs shoving cameras and microphones in her face and sirens wailing in her ears. The sound had awakened her and she saw the fire trucks and police cars converge around the throng of vehicles. They were actually driving on the sidewalks since there was nowhere for the many cars to go. Nearly an hour had passed and she wondered what they would do next. She decided to entrust these two men with her safety and comfort until their situation changed and she could resume control of her own destiny. She tried to doze off again.

As the evening progressed Bella was getting annoyed that wherever she went, Alice was a few steps behind. Bella went to see Rebecca to ask for news. And Alice pulled up alongside her to eavesdrop. Bella checked in with the news media feed people and Alice stepped up and interjected *her* apology that Orinthbey couldn't be there for the live broadcast. Then she elaborated about the Ivory Coast situation. The pool reporter asked her why she, Alice, and Bella were not helping the President deal with the Ivory Coast situation. Bella beat Alice to the punch this time, "The President is on a private call at the moment with the ambassador. Apparently there are personal elements to this crisis, which require the utmost discretion. As you may have noticed, it's now 7:00 p.m. and we are still at the White House standing by for whatever the President needs when he calls upon us." Bella turned and walked away hoping that *this* time Alice would follow her. Instead Alice remained with the pool reporter to ingratiate herself. Bella's irritation quickened her pace. She returned to her office and sat down behind her desk. For this moment of privacy she called her Deputy at Intelligence. "What have you learned?"

"First, about the Evans person. Yes, he is well connected. We followed him out of there and picked up a transmission of some set of cryptic digitized messages. We believe he was making contact of some sort. We did pick up the audible, 'Negative 1 will commence shortly.' We don't know what that is but we suspect the attack on the President is what they are referring to."

"Have you got the FBI on this? If you have enough, you need to arrest him. And it sounds like you have enough to bring him in."

"Yes, I have the FBI here now. They also have the inside news on the President's condition. They pumped his stomach, the blood work is affirmative: he was poisoned. It appears that the agent causes paralysis. They are keeping his vitals functioning, all by machines. He won't be back to action tonight. It will be a while before he could return. We are lucky the chef was with him and hit the panic button as fast as he had. If the medics were any later, he'd be dead."

She inhaled audibly and asked, "So what about the investigation?"

"Well, like I said the Chef saved his life. Though he seems the only logical suspect at this time because of access to the food and to the President, it's obviously too obvious. We're working on him now to recall anyone or anything out of the ordinary in the kitchen. I'm guessing this Kale guy has someone on the inside that no one suspects."

"Try Roullin. He's been meeting with Kale regularly on official business. It's in the logs. Plus Kale was here meeting with him this afternoon before he saw the President."

"Really?"

"Yes, Evans was here for a meeting and asked Rebecca to see Orinthbey unappointed. Percival met with him this afternoon."

"That means there are tapes of their conversation. I'll get Weatherby to check their conversation. And I'll have his team scrub the room they met in, was it the Oval?"

"Yes, it was the Oval office. I'll let Weatherby and his team in."

"Good. We'll solve this, Bella. Call me again in 15."

"Thanks Manning."

Bella knew that Alice would want to be sworn in if she heard this same news. She had to put off Alice as long as possible and keep Alice isolated. She needed some busy-work for Alice to do. She decided to call Ricardo.

"Yes, Madame Secretary," Ricardo answered the phone with eminence.

"Hi Ricardo. I need your help."

"Of course, Ms. Gliad, what can I do?"

"Madame Vice President has been following me around all evening. I know she's worried about the President; she's worried about what the future brings. You know her best, though. What would be the best way to occupy her vast intellect and her concern until we know more about the President and our days ahead? Would she be most interested in being briefed on everything to keep her mind off her worries? Or would she be better served with some sort of *distraction*?"

Ricardo wondered then how much Bella Gliad knew. "Madame Vice President is a complex woman. Her interests are widespread. Though I know her *best*, I cannot speculate on her state of mind at this moment and how best to put her concerns at rest."

"Well, for the good of our Country, would you please find out and *accommodate* her? If she wants the briefings I have Jesse from Staff standing by in the blue salon waiting to brief both of you on everything. He has a general presentation he gives, which he can drill down on topics of interest into great detail. Or, if you prefer, the Staff has the Lincoln *bedroom* ready for the Vice President and its adjoining quarters ready for yourself, Ricardo. Please get her settled either way. We should know more about the President's condition in about an hour." Ricardo heard her emphasize the word "bedroom".

"I will be happy to serve my Country, Madame Secretary, in either capacity." And he hung up.

She headed over to the Station and collected Weatherby and his team. They marched through the halls to the Oval. She called Rebecca on the way to tell her a team investigating any signs that would explain the President's illness. Rebecca greeted the team when they arrived and pointed to the frappucino cup the President was drinking from earlier in the afternoon. She closed the door to give the team privacy during their investigation.

FOURTEEN
Monday Evening, Georgetown

The phone rang, vibrating in his shirt pocket. He slipped it out of his pocket while he held up his hand to his dinner companion and left the table to attend to his conversation near the entrance to the men's room at Epicurean's near her apartment in Georgetown. She looked on with curiosity as he left their table. They had been dating for just 2 weeks and she was hoping he was the one. She was in her last year at Georgetown and wanted to be married by the time she graduated. He was attending the A. James Clark School of Engineering at the University of Maryland to study mechanical engineering and she admired his intelligence and thought his career would be a good complement to her own in political science. Though he had seemed interested in her, he hadn't revealed much about himself yet in their blossoming friendship.

He returned to the table and said he had a family emergency he had to go home to deal with. She gave him a concerned look, searching his face for answers. She was too shy to ask such a bold question as what was wrong so instead she said, "Is there anything I can do to help?"

As he laid a $100 bill on the table and reached for her hand, he gave her an odd smile and replied, "I wish there were, but I should only be gone for the night and back tomorrow. It's not that bad, just a dear friend of my mom's needs my help tonight," as he leaned down to give her a quick kiss good-night. He knew she was just 21 and crazy for him. He was just 3 years older and about to finish his master's degree in mechanical engineering. He already had a double-major in electrical and computer engineering from Boston College. He once had plans to work for NASA or one of its contractors and knew his shoe-in was his three diplomas, top grades, and his earlier internships with NASA and with Lockheed-Martin. He had wanted to work on space-based systems in the space station, satellites, or space defense systems. He had shared this much with Kelly but she kept pressing him for more about himself.

He walked her to her dormitory where she gave him a long kiss, "Good night, Jason". He sighed and then headed for his car. He lived about 30 miles away and was fortunate to have a car to use. But he didn't head back to his apartment this evening. Instead he drove east to Chinatown where he parked his car on the street in front of a restaurant, 186. He grabbed his book bag from the front seat of his car, stepped out and locked the car doors and walked inside. He sat at the counter and ordered a Tsing-Tao and two egg rolls. While he waited for his egg rolls to be cooked, he slipped into the men's room and changed his clothes from his tan blazer and slacks into jeans and a baggy sweatshirt. He quickly swallowed the food and beer, paid his bill, and dropped a $20 on the table. He then exited out the rear of the restaurant. He went down an alley, found a narrow staircase, climbed the stairs and went into a tiny studio apartment. The apartment was dark. It had one small window opposite the entry door. Next to the window was a mini-refrigerator upon which sat a toaster oven. Next to it was a tiny stainless steel sink set into a production-made cabinet with 12 inches of countertop on either side. Three shelves stood above the entire kitchen with bowls, cups, and Cheerios lining their space. By the entry door and opposite this kitchen was a tiny bathroom: a shower in a corner, a toilet in the other corner, and a small sink by the door.

He stepped inside the bathroom for a moment and splashed cold water on his face, slicked back his hair with water and glued it in place with hair gel. He then reached into a wide-mouthed jar of a jelly-like substance. It was gritty and sandy to the touch. He grabbed a few tablespoons with his right hand, pressed it into his left hand, spread it among his fingers, and smacked the substance onto his clean-shaven face. The result was amazing – he appeared to have a thin beard now. The gritty substance composed of small hairs he had previously shaven from his face, now coming to life again.

He stepped out of the small bathroom and took three steps to reach the open side of the room, where a small closet stood in its corner. He unlocked the locks that he kept on the closet door and reached in to grab a shirt, pants, and a hat all hanging on a single hanger. He changed his baggy sweater for a black long-sleeve Under Armour shirt. He took off the jeans and replaced them with the black Craghoppers pants. He hung his jeans and sweater onto the now empty hanger and replaced it in the closet. He swapped his loafers for black sneakers in the closet. He placed a black plain ball cap on his head. He reached up to the shelf and grabbed a backpack and a hip bag. He belted the hip bag onto his waist. Then he fastened straps from the hip bag around his thighs, to fashion a climbing harness. Finally he rolled the backpack onto his shoulders. Then he reached into the back of the closet and grabbed the main switch the circuit breaker panel and moved it to the "off" position. His clock went dim and the one small light was now off. He reached into his hip bag and pulled out a headlamp which he placed on his head, over his cap and turned on to a low-light emitting red glow.

He stepped out the window onto a fire escape and he climbed up to the roof. He walked across the roof to the next building and walked across it. He then opened the roof access door and walked down the stairs to the main level. He walked out to the street and headed east 3 blocks. There was a parking lot that surrounded a cell/radio tower. The parking lot was surrounded by a chain link fence lined with barbed wire. He headed to the northwest corner of the parking lot. He pulled out his wire cutters from his backpack and went to work cutting a small hole near the ground, only big enough to let a 70 pound dog through. He shoved his gear into the hole and then slid through face down, feet first, until he was through. He grabbed some leaves and twigs that had piled up in the corner and covered his opening as he walked along the fence until he was centered along its northern edge. There were two outbuildings between him and the tower on this side. The parking lot was alight but it didn't seem anyone was watching. Nevertheless, Jason wasn't taking any chances. He pulled a black cape from his backpack and a can of spray glue. He gathered more fallen brown leaves from the ground. He sprayed the aerosol glue onto the cape and spread the leaves over it. He put the glue back in his pack and spread the cape over his head and pack. He moved slowly across the parking lot to the first outbuilding. There was dark cover here as he moved stealthily to the second outbuilding and into the light again. Here he moved the loose fence away from the building and pressed himself in the narrow opening. He looked up at the tower.

He set his cape down on the ground among the other leaves. He swung a hook from his hip bag to the bottom rung of the ladder, which was a few feet over his head. Because his pack was harnessed around his waist and between his legs, as he pushed a button to engage a retractor he was lifted up to the ladder. He began the long, slow climb up the tower, attaching and detaching his harness at each level.

The steel lattice tower had been constructed during the 1950s as a radio tower in the heyday of radio. It served the greater Capital area for the entire time. In the early 1980s it was the first of seven towers in the Capital area to be fitted with the new-age cellular telephone network transceiver. It had been upgraded more times than any other tower in the nation with the newest and latest transceivers. It continually broadcasted AM radio signals as well and served as a support tower for the FAA in monitoring air traffic in the region.

During Jason's undergraduate studies at Boston, he wrote a paper about the tower, adding to its fame. He met with the people that maintained and managed the tower while spending a summer internship working on it doing maintenance. He got to change the light bulbs at the top of the tower, applied special coatings to the metal work and did tests to see if the metal's strength was compromised underneath the coatings. He also helped install new antennae and a weather monitoring system to it during his summer internship.

Now he was scaling the tower for the last time. The peak height a human can reach on the tower is 350 feet. That was his destination. He was fulfilling his destiny. He was part of a mission to remake his country in a dramatic way. And the beauty was no one would be hurt. It would take him another hour to reach the summit and he spent this time thinking about the next days, weeks, and months.

The first $500,000 payment had been deposited into his account weeks ago. Tomorrow he would check that the second $500,000 was deposited. Then he would finish writing his thesis, *Protection Means and Methods of Solid State Devices from Coronal Mass Ejection-Induced Electromagnetic Pulse Interference.* He would be a hot commodity after tonight. He had developed insulation technologies and methods to protect solid state devices. He had looked into Faraday cages but they were expensive and didn't insulate in all directions. Tonight several devices would be tested. He loved his work. And he loved his country. He would bring about the kind of change that was needed. No more of these cronies, all of the same stripe, going to war in far-off places, giving away massive foreign aid. Free college tuition for everyone. It was time for more fairness. He joined a change-group called *Fair Nation*. Their mission was to promote change in our society so that the world could be fairer. Fairness in education of all children, all the way through college. Fairness in the job market so all people could work. Fairness in how people are treated. It had sounded good to him as an undergraduate in Boston. His whole dormitory had signed up when their R.A. came to talk about the organization. Jason joined. He didn't have to give money. He just had to go once per month to help out at various events. Then he got the call from the State Director of *Fair Nation* that he could be funded in his graduate studies in exchange for working more events. He needed the money and signed up willingly. His college loans from Boston were paid off for him as he worked events, his graduate studies were paid for and the events work actually benefitted his studies, culminating in his research project and this test.

If things kept going well between him and Kelly, he would marry her. She was sweet, smart, and adored him. That would work. He would become the world's foremost expert on preventing damage to electronic devices – a huge market and an endless outlook, especially after tonight. He needed a wife to get to the next level respectably.

As he reached the pinnacle of the tower, he secured his lines and leaned back. He attached his backpack to the wire. He reached in and pulled out a metal box, about the size of a 4 slice toaster. On the side of the box he had inscribed Marx II on it. He laughed to himself. Marx generators had been invented by German Erwin Otto Marx in 1924 to produce high voltage electrical pulses. Marx generators were used 40 years ago in pulsed electron beam generators to simulate lightning so its effects could be studied more closely. They had only recently been perfected and applied to propagate pulses to generate powerful X-rays, simulate coronal ejections, and trigger massive chain reactions. Adding highly reactive chemicals to chambers in the Marx II initiated the reaction that would be propagated and amplified into a concentrated beam generating a single maximum pulse of energy. This size box could generate a significant pulse to cover a five mile radius with a less-intense pulse extended another 5 miles beyond. It was symbolic that it had the same name of the 19th century father of radical communism, Karl Marx.

The Marx II had knobs and lights on it. He tied it to the line in three places. Then he fastened some wired connectors from the box to both sides of the tower's support. He double and triple checked the connections. Then he flipped a switch and the LED alighted. Next he moved some dials and the indicators responded. He pressed one more button that illuminated a timer. It started counting down from 2 hours. Jason took a minute to enjoy the view. The Capitol was alight in the distance. The White House could be seen from here, between himself and the Capitol. The Washington monument looked down, even upon him at this height. And the city was beautiful. He said good-bye to the Tower and said 'See you later' to the City. He put his backpack back on and set about climbing down the tower. After he climbed down he retraced his steps out of the parking lot, back to the alley, into his apartment, changing his clothes. He went down the stairs and out to the street to his car since 186, the Chinese restaurant, was closed now. He drove west without looking back. He looked at his watch. He had about 15 minutes left to gain as much distance as he could. He found his way to I-66 and drove toward the Shenandoah mountains. He texted his contact, "done".

FIFTEEN
Early Tuesday Past Midnight, Cocoa, Florida

Surprisingly, Jake did not feel sleepy. After he pulled the car into the dirt parking lot of Salty's marina overflow area, he ran his fingers through his crew-style hair cut to stimulate the scalp over his brain to get his mind to shift gears from driving all night to loading up the yacht. In the dark of the car, he spent a moment texting his in-laws to let them know he and Mari were here. They would be driving over with the children in the early morning to meet them. Jake nudged Mari awake and asked her to walk with him to *Point of Departure* and get on board. When he stepped out of the rental car, into the crisp, cool night air, he felt exhilarated. The stars were twinkling above and he looked up to them and said a small prayer of thanks for their safe arrival here and for the wisdom to make the next adventure a safe and good one.

He collected Mari, went to their slip in the water, brought her on board, unlocked the cabin, and put her to bed in the captain's berth. He returned to the car and collected the rest of her things. Then he joined her on board and laid himself down for a nice sleep. He could rest the next several hours before they had to shove off. He put his arm around his wife's waist as she slept and he felt overcome with the emotions of the last few days. A huge weight left his body and he floated on the gentle water to a deep sleep.

The sky had cleared and the stars were making an appearance. The calm of the sky contrasted with the surface of the Earth in this place. The center of power for the entire world belonged here, inside these stately structures of marble by masters of architecture. It had only suffered wounds of significance three times in its two centuries: the War of 1812 when several buildings, including the White House, Capitol and War Department, were burned by the British in a raid; during the Civil War when Confederate General Jubal Early attacked Fort Stevens nearly injuring President Lincoln. Though Early retreated within days, all construction on the Washington monument was halted and its balance of power was questioned by the blood of its countrymen; and third, when pirates of the high sky tore through its space and wounded its face of honor on 9/11/2001 at the Pentagon. A half century from now the grandchildren-historians will see this day as the fourth time that it suffered the vindictive, belligerent, and defiling nature of some men. The future historian would hopefully contrast these four events and expose the differences as well: the marauders' torment in 1814, the consequences of the need for domination over others in 1864, in 2001 the pestiferous evil of sharia, and now the collection of takers defacing and destroying the symbols of the system that generously gave to them. The excess wealth of free markets bred the takers, whom could not see their goal was nihilistic.

Her feet and legs were cold and she awoke abruptly. She quickly assessed that she was still in Congressman Blanzing's limousine. He was asleep, so was J.B., and as best she could tell, so was the driver. The car was not running, but the lights were on. She decided it must be between 50 and 60 degrees in the car, which was in the middle of Jefferson Davis Parkway just north of Alexandria. Everywhere she looked there were cars stopped in the road. Her watch said 3:55 a.m. She tapped J.B.'s arm and whispered, "J.B., wake up!"

He made a small sound and slowly moved his eyes until they opened. "It's 4 in the morning and the car isn't running and we're stuck in the middle of a highway."

He looked around and climbed out of the car. She followed him out. There were a few people milling about along the sidewalks; others were walking south. Jasmine heard some whimpering and soft crying sounds in the distance. The clear, cold night helped the sound travel farther. As she turned full circle she could see the light of flames coming from near the capital. "Look."

J.B.'s brain cleared quickly in the cold air. He assessed the flames and muttered, "It must have been a real bomb threat that evacuated us." He leaned in the car and woke up Ray and the driver. J.B. shut the door again to retain the heat in the interior but could still overhear the driver apologizing that he fell asleep. The car was still running last he knew, but pointing to the shifter, showed that it was in park. He relayed to Ray that the gas tank had been full when they left the previous night. Ray was opening the door as the driver was still saying, "I left the engine idling for the heat, even though we were only moving less than one mile per hour all night. I last remember seeing the clock at 2 something."

Ray turned back and poked his face into the car, "You did just fine, Roman; thank you."

Ray saw the sky to the north and knew that the situation was bad. He tried to call some colleagues but the cell towers must not have been working because he couldn't get any signal at all. He started shaking his head in disbelief. A burdened sadness warped the creases in his face.

Jasmine spoke first, "Look, we shouldn't stay here. If the phones are out and the city is burning, it won't be long until bad people start preying on the good people. We need to *survive*. We do that by taking charge of our situation. Is there any way we can fly out of here? The airport is that way, right?" she pointed toward Reagan National Airport.

J.B. looked that direction. The airport was dark. He couldn't see the tower. There was no sound of jet engines. "Doubtful."

"Shall we try it or shall we head south on foot?"

The driver climbed out of the car with a look of fear on his face. "Sir, may I have a word?"

Ray walked over to the driver where they had a private conversation. When he returned, Jasmine look straight at the driver and asked, "What supplies of water and snacks are in the car?" He popped open the trunk, which held a cooler full of purified water, some boxes of cheese, and a satchel of cracker packets. He pointed to the red box in the corner with First Aid supplies. Jasmine grabbed it all and handed out the supplies for each of the 4 of them to carry. "Drink when you are thirsty. Don't wait for us to find more water. To keep warm, we will walk arm in arm."

She reached for her pocketknife, which was not there because the TSA won't allow law-abiders to carry survival tools with them when traveling by air. She looked at Roman while asking, "Who has a knife?"

Then J.B. reminded her, "You bought one today from Mike, remember?"

She decided she was more tired than she felt. J.B. leaned into the car and removed a large black bag. He pulled out a sturdy shopping bag that had her purchases in it. She reached into the bag and found the knife, still in its box. She pulled out the *Benchmade Mel Pardue* stainless steel knife and sliced the lining of the back side of her jacket so that it formed a pocket, like a backpack. She put her share of supplies in it. She held up the knife for the others, "Who wants to do the same? It saves your hands and shields your supply from the view of looters."

J.B. went next, then Ray. Roman had a man-purse already on his arm. Jasmine drank some water from her bottle, courtesy of the limo, and put it away. She asked Roman for matches, a lighter, flashlights, plastic ware, cups, and so forth. She pulled out everything and set it on the hood of the car. She took her knife and cut away part of the fabric backing of two of the seats in the limo to make shoulder-bags in which to put these other supplies. She loaded them up until their weight was about even and announced they would take turns carrying the bags.

"All we have left to do is decide what our destination is. Who lives close by? Is there gasoline and a car we could get to? If we can't fly is there another mode we can use to leave the area? What about the train stations – Metro or Amtrak?"

Roman said he couldn't help. He lived east in Maryland countryside. J.B. didn't have much here. He used his limo to get around when he left the city, and stayed in his office or a nearby hotel when he was here. "We can check the Metro. But it's electric and the power seems to be not working everywhere. Look around. It's doubtful we can travel by the Metro. And the Amtrak station is another 15 miles south of here."

Ray had an apartment in the city but nothing away from it. Except, "I have a trawler we can use. It's moored near here – about a couple of miles ahead, south of Alexandria in Belle Haven."

"Sounds good. Lead the way;" ordered Jasmine, adding "let's stay on the main road for now, so long as there are still regular people about us."

Before setting off, J.B. looked behind them at the city. The fires were still raging. He looked around at the people near them and determined they must all have left the city around the same time last night. He was curious what news there was. How bad was this? Were the firefighters putting the fires out? What was the President's condition? How come the cell towers weren't working near here? He shivered, turned and jogged to join up with his group, and pulled himself close to Jasmine as they locked arms. The four of them were almost comically marching to the Emerald City to see the Wizard himself.

Nearly an hour later they had made it south near to the center of Alexandria. Roman had been slowing them down with numerous complaints. Now he was shivering and taking a moment to vomit on the sidewalk. The sky was still dark. The numbers of people walking the same path had diminished and Jasmine's spine was prickling with apprehension that they had the appearance of prey to predators. Predators know how to pick off the easiest victims. "It's time to get off the Parkway. How much farther, Ray?"

"Good, Jasmine, because to get to the dock most efficiently, we should head through that neighborhood," he said as he pointed eastward. "We'll walk three blocks east, then take Washington street south, under the overpass, and along the golf course to get to the marina."

The streetlights weren't working so she had no idea what he was pointing toward, other than a gray silhouette of buildings. "Roman, are you ready? We need to push on!"

Roman was overweight and spent too much time behind the wheel of a car, and not enough time using his muscles. Now he was ill. He was making them vulnerable. He didn't respond but for a whimper.

"Roman, it's much safer for us if we keep moving."

"She's right, Roman, we need you to pull yourself together and at least keep walking," J.B. chimed in.

Ray had been holding his own. Though he had his own survival training, he didn't work out enough and he didn't keep updated. He regretted now that his life was a bit too cushy. At least he trusted J.B. from their work over the past 4 years. And he trusted Jasmine just by how she handled herself. She clearly had some clues about survival and he was grateful she was leading them. "Roman, please help us help you."

At this Roman lifted himself up off the curb, his eyes were welling up with tears and he started whimpering, "I'm so sorry, Mr. Blanzing, I'm so sorry."

Blanzing thought Roman was overreacting about their urging him to keep moving. J.B. noticed this, too, but thought for different reasons. "Roman, is there something you're not telling us?"

Roman just cried louder and couldn't speak from his gasping.

J.B. searched Ray's face for a clue. Then he looked at Jasmine. She spoke up now. "Look, I know you're sorry Roman. But we are not going to *survive* out here if you keep making so much noise. You have to get a hold of yourself or we will have to go separate ways," as she slightly shook his shoulders. His crying eased a bit.

Blanzing now started to think that this Jasmine was perhaps overdoing it. Was the threat to leave Roman serious? Perhaps she was being too harsh on him. Blanzing started to walk toward Roman to help him along but as he approached, a fast-approaching shadow startled him backward and he caught himself before tripping.

The sounds quickly succeeded each other in a few instants. First was the snap of a twig, then the sound of a small object sliding across a leather strap a few inches, a wince, then the sound of a hammer cocking on a small, solid revolver, then a gagging and a gurgle, another slip of metal across a leather strap, and the sound of a semi-automatic handgun being racked, followed by a ripping noise and accelerating footsteps of descending pitch, as the soft-footed predator ran away. The last sound was Blanzing wrestling the flashlight from his jacket pouch and shining it on the scene. There lay Roman in a pool of blood. He had been stabbed. His jacket was gone from his back, and his wallet torn from his pants.

"Shine it down there!" Jasmine aimed down the street. Blanzing complied. They could see a short man trotting away at the end of the street a block away. Jasmine thought about approaching him, but realized he would be back with a few more predators, just the paltry reward of some coats, supplies, and cash.

Their eyes all pointed down to Roman's body. J.B. knelt down and reached for a pulse. The blood was spreading across the pavement as Ray shone the light on his face.

J.B. looked up at them and shook his head. Then turning back to Roman he said, "Can you hear me, Roman?"

There was no response. No fluttering eyes. No sign he was conscious. J.B. touched his neck and said, "I can't feel a pulse. And I don't think he's breathing." He stood up to whisper to the other two, "He can't be dead. Not yet, at least."

Ray showed his first sign of emotion of the evening just now. It was the agitation that comes from helplessness. "What are going to do? We can't carry him. We can't leave him," as he kept shaking his head in disbelief.

Jasmine could feel a wall rising around her. She could not lose focus of getting to safety. She leaned over to Ray and put her hand on his shoulder as she whispered, "Ray, that guy will be back with others. We need to get to safety before anything else. Let's turn off the light but carry it in your front pocket. We'll walk in a line so that we don't shoot each other for one getting in front of another. They will be back with enough power to take what we have and to take our lives. They have proven it right in front of our eyes." She paused to let this sink in. "We need to hide for a time or backtrack to avoid a confrontation. Which do you choose?"

Both J.B. and Blanzing were weary now. J.B. offered, "The sun should be up in about an hour. Do you want to hole up somewhere until then?"

"Ok. We passed by a storefront one block back. Let's go and hide there."

She led the way. It was a child's toy store. She used Blanzing's flashlight to head down into the space behind the buildings as she tried doors and windows in the back alley. "We can break in, or we can hide behind the dumpster.

Which is it men?" Both of them had looks of repulsion at the suggestion of hiding in a dark alley behind a smelly dumpster. They were as abhorred by the notion of breaking into a building. They both stared at her blankly.

"Gentlemen, may I remind you our survival is at stake? If I must, I will choose for you." She was thinking of the *normalcy bias* that sets in with most people when all is not normal. People try to act like life is still normal. It's *normal* to respect the law and not to break into places to hide. But it isn't normal to have all the power and cell phones not working, to have all traffic seized for several hours and to have the Nation's capital burning. She didn't have time to explain that to them now. She had to help them find a lifeboat, a literal lifeboat.

J.B. coughed and asked, "Which do *you* choose?"

"The smelly alley because we can bug out easier from there. Look, one of us can watch from up there." She pointed to a narrow roof over the loading dock on the next building.

The men thought it better than committing a felony breaking into a business for their safety so they agreed. She had them hide behind the dumpster and announced she would take the first shift of 20-25 minutes while the two men napped. Neither man felt like he could sleep but both welcomed a chance to get off their feet. They sat in their business suits on some pieces of cardboard they found and propped their feet up against the dumpster, to prevent Charlie-horses from forming in their legs. Lactic acid can build up in the muscle tissue if exercise is done without breathing properly and resting often enough. She climbed up on the roof and lay on her belly watching the opposite end of the alley.

She tried to get a signal on her phone. Nothing. She didn't have a radio on her and there was none in the car when they packed up. There was no way yet to know what was happening and how bad it was. She shook her head and wondered what just happened in the past 12 hours.

Her shift was quiet. After 20 minutes, she quietly climbed down from her perch. She walked around their hideout to see if anyone was around. She reached the end of the alley and sidled up to the corner of the brick building to have a peak into the main street. A block down was a city green and there were 4 or 5 guys sitting on the stone wall that surrounds the green space. Two were smoking and another was talking.

She peered with her ears cupped by her hands. "…blasted… smoke…. ran up to….nope, no cell phones… yeah, I know what that means…. wreck the place… wreck everything… no, no killing but they'll be dead anyway… dead anyway… get out of the way… sure, always wanted to… now?.... go find some now…. It's our turn, ha ha ha ha, hee ha."

Jasmine didn't like the sound of that. She went back quietly to wake up Ray and J.B. She whispered, "A gang of hoodlums are a block away. Sounds like they want to kill and loot for the fun of it." She turned her head toward the bright light of an approaching police car along the main street out from their alley. She had a moment of hope. Blanzing pronounced, "Now, it's not so bad!" and started to proudly march toward the end of the street.

"Wait!" Jasmine whisper-yelled. She caught up to him and grabbed his arm. "Watch before you go out there."

The three of them found her peering place at the front of the alley. The police car pulled up to the hoodlums and sounded its siren in a series of whoops and gurgles. The hoodlums just laughed. Blanzing made a face of disbelief. The driver got out of the car, and drawled, "Lookie what I caught. I got me a po-leese car. Now we is the law. Heh heh heh." There were knuckle bumps and butt-bumps and fancy handshake smacks. The gang all piled into the car. On the passenger side, as one hoodlum opened the door, a limp police officer slumped sideways toward the street. The hoodlum grabbed his shirt by the neck and dumped the body onto the street. He picked his pockets and grabbed a nightstick.

This time Jasmine felt the panic rise up in her throat and she wanted to vomit. But she tilted her head back to repress the urge. She raced quietly to the back door of the toy store and shoved her hand into the window. She opened the door and the three of them went inside. She grabbed phone books and shoved them in their shirts. She spoke clearly and quietly: "Grab any fire extinguishers you can find." She saw a radio and she turned it on. Nothing but static. She wondered how that could be. She found some kids' cameras for sale. "Look, unwrap all these cameras." She ripped open a couple of the packages and J.B. helped her with the rest. "The flash will temporarily blind the attackers. Use them as defensive weapons." She peaked from the window and saw the police car turnaround at the end of the street and head back toward her building. She backed away from the window. The driver floored the engine. The car headed up the hill and out of town, toward the highway. She waited. "Ok. We have to find a way to carry all this stuff." She pressed a button and a bright flash made her leather-seat cover bag light up on the inside. "Practice on a camera each so you know what to do in the dark."

As Ray and J.B. each tried a camera in the bag they were sharing, they watched as Jazz headed to the shop's checkout counter. She disappeared behind it and they could hear her retching into the trash pail. She said a small prayer and wiped her mouth with some paper. She took a swig of water. Her bottle was almost empty. "Ready? Let's go."

SIXTEEN

Tuesday Morning, Alexandria, Virginia

Their walk through and out of town was uneventful. It was still mostly dark but there was a slight glow over the water to the east. From within the trees across the park from the marina, Ray was pointing to the dock where his yacht was moored.

J.B. announced, "It will take us a few minutes to walk across that expanse and about a minute to run it. How well are you both holding up?"

Neither Ray nor Jasmine responded. They were both tired.

"Ok. I'm just asking because if anyone is watching us or has been following us, we will be exposed going across this field and they could catch up to us or climb aboard before we can get underway. So we need to rest here until we're ready to make a run for it. Then we need to be ready to pull off as soon as we climb aboard. How long does it take to get underway, Ray?"

Blanzing paused to think, "I usually spend a few minutes blowing out vapors before starting the engine. While I'm doing that my crew is stowing gear, disconnecting shore power and shore water, and then standing by to toss the lines when I pull away. I guess that's usually 10 minutes but I suppose we could cut and run in about 2 minutes, still a long time."

Jasmine spoke up now, "If there is someone pursuing us, does it make sense to wait here and let them catch up and rest up? And wouldn't it be likely that they're faster than us?" She tried not to look at Ray Blanzing at that moment. Though he was in great health for his age, he was still in his 60s, leading to the logical conclusion he would be a slower runner than a 20 year old thug.

Ray spoke up now. "We have three choices: stay here indefinitely, cross the field now, or cross the field later. I don't like any of those choices. I think if we keep walking south, beyond the marina, and get closer to the waterfront, we can then backtrack up along the boats along the water's edge. We'll have the boats for cover and can move forward more tactically, one at a time, splitting up and watching each other."

Before J.B. could comment, Jasmine said, "Let's do it."

J.B. blinked at her. And decided he'd go along. He got up and started walking.

The long way around added 15 minutes to their trip and added to their fatigue. But they were able to keep their eyes on the woods behind them, using the sea wall, moored yachts, and marina effects as cover. No one was on their trail as they reached Blanzing's yacht, *Patriot*, so they breathed a sigh of relief. Ray started the blowers as soon as he reached the helm. J.B. disconnected shore power and water and Jasmine grabbed the binoculars in the box and monitored their surroundings. Two minutes later Blanzing started the engine and J.B. loosed the bow lines. After J.B. stepped back aboard, he turned around and large, aged bare feet appeared in front of him.

J.B. stammered, "Hi."

Jasmine turned around from her watch of the shore. Where did this fellow come from?

Ray called out quickly, "Hi Kenny! How ya doin?"

Jasmine and J.B. exchanged concerned looks.

"Hi Ray. What brings you out here on a Tuesday?" Kenny drew out the 'Tue' in Tuesday, sounding like 'Toosday'.

"Well, there's been a commotion in the capital so we left for a while to go for a ride. It's a bit cold, but we wanted the fresh air."

"Hmmph," replied the salty, trim, tanned, and wrinkled fisherman. "Not much to see today. But best to ya."

Ray queried, "Any news today, Kenny?"

Kenny just waved his hand toward their boat in disgust and continued to walk back to his yacht two bays down.

Ray raised his eyebrows and called down to J.B., "Loose the stern lines!"

J.B. quickly loosed the lines and announced, "Aye, aye, captain. Stern lines loosed."

Ray eased the yacht forward. Jasmine kept her watch on the trees and the shoreline. Then she looked toward Kenny as he waved from the bow of his yacht. She waved. He waved back and called out, "News is country is a mess. An absolute mess. Why ain't you fixin' it, Congressman?"

Ray called back, "I'm working it every single day. An endless uphill climb."

Patriot maneuvered about the various moorings to the harbor's egress and bound out to the pitching waterway. Jasmine went below and found some windbreakers and sweatshirts. She put on a sweatshirt. Then she slid a windbreaker on over top. She brought the others to J.B. and Ray. Jasmine pulled out cameras that Ray had on board so they could record the scene. She saw there were provisions and fresh water aboard and grabbed some packs of crackers and dried fruit for them to snack on. She started a pot of coffee in the galley. She said a quick prayer to give thanks for this moment of peace. They all sat on the flybridge behind the clear, vinyl windbreaks to look out on the shore. Ray turned north so they could survey the damage in Washington.

As they headed north on the Potomac River they could see a cloud of smoke moving east across the sky. Ray was trying the AM radio, the GPS, the satellite weather station, and his VHF radio. The AM was all static. The GPS was working fine. Satellite weather was showing overcast skies but no foul weather. And he could hear other boaters on the VHF. He listened to the other boaters to hear about the news.

She shivered for a moment. Then felt the hand of her cameraman shaking her shoulder. "Namia, wake up!"

Namia Pruvati woke up slowly and remembered how she came to be sleeping in the news van with her cameraman last evening. She had been reporting from the studio about the President falling ill and got the call from Jasmine Roberts that there were police cars and fire trucks all around the Capitol. She and her cameraman decided to come out to the scene to investigate and report. They had tried to interview several emergency officials and got no new information. They filmed the blazing lights and crowded roads for a few hours, checking in for a live report every half hour or so. At 11:00 o'clock they were ready to go back to the studio in Northern Virginia for the night. But their local channel warned them that the traffic was completely jammed to the south and east of the Capitol and they should head west before coming south to Arlington. They climbed into their van, which was parked at 3rd and Independence to head west on Independence. The traffic was still heavy but they were making headway. Namia was turning on the van's radio to listen to some music and get a few moments rest from the endless news cycle.

She felt a pain in her forehead and realized her eyes were squeezed shut, without being conscious of this. She tried to open them but they still hurt. A moment later there was a deafening sound and she pressed her hands to her ears to protect them. She heard Shaun, the cameraman, exclaim, "What the hell?"

Then a moment later it was over. Except for a slight ringing in her ears, it was eerily quiet. Namia wondered if her eardrums were blown out. But Shaun said, "What was that?" Namia shook her head in disbelief. She reached to turn on the radio to get a news report or an emergency signal, the knob was warm to the touch and indicated the radio was *on* though no sound was coming. She blinked. She looked at the van door and saw a small puff of smoke coming from the embedded speaker. Shaun tried all the knobs and buttons on their expensive transmission and recording equipment. Everything was dead, some of it was warm, some of it was smoking. And he smelled the smell of fried electrical equipment. He went to start the engine of the van, but the key was still in the "on" position. Murmuring to himself, "How can this be?"

Namia registered all this, "It must be an EMP, an electro-magnetic pulse. It kills all electronic devices, fries the wiring, fries circuit boards, overloads batteries, which damages them, everything." She pulled out her cell phone; it wasn't responding. "Not my phone, too!" She thought about this some more. An EMP meant no transportation, no communication, no way to return to the studio. She looked out the van window.

Though Namia was not from a wealthy family, she was accustomed to having everything clean, neat, and perfect. She spent her free time in malls, libraries, and bookstores, never in the outdoors. She didn't like boating, hiking, jogging, and would never dream of camping. She preferred nicer hotels, room service, the health club, and fashion. So she sat there pondering how on earth she could get from this stranded van to the ECF Studio, or to her apartment, without being in the cold night air, in the darkness, away from the comforts of her life.

Shaun knew Namia really well. He knew her preferences. As an outdoor guy himself, he knew there were people of different walks – outdoorsy or not. He dated enough girls of both sorts that he could size them up quickly by their walk, the way they wear their hair, what shoes they wear, their nails, and what they carry. An outdoorsy girl has simple, easy to take care of hair. She wears shoes she can walk in easily for a long mile, her nails are not grotesquely long and flamboyant, and she walks in a steady pace, as one would have to for a long haul. The glamorous girls have the fluffy, expensive haircuts, the jeweled nails, the stiletto heels, the gait that comes from wearing high heels too much, and, believe it or not, they giggle more. He liked working with Namia, but she was a glamour girl all the way. He didn't know too many outdoorsy girls that go in front of cameras – their looks are too plain for the camera. He decided, while considering this, that they would both be better off, staying overnight in the van, at least until the light of day could help.

He pulled out his duffle bag from behind the driver seat. He had two emergency blankets in it, two bottles of water, a small first aid kit, two small but high intensity flashlights, a headlamp for him, two packs of canned shoestring potato sticks, and a small AM radio. The radio wasn't working. He opened the battery compartment and saw the batteries were enlarged. But he handed Namia a water bottle, one can of potato sticks, and a flashlight. "We'll have to sleep in here for the night. We can't call anyone or drive anywhere. So our choices are to walk to Virginia or to sleep in here. There is room in here for both of us and I bet you don't have walking shoes, so let's camp out here and decide what to do in the morning, okay?"

Namia appreciated the solid confidence of Shaun's voice. She knew him well, too, and knew that she could trust him. She was grateful she was not alone. She pressed the on button of her flashlight. Nothing happened, "I guess these are useless, too," as she tossed it back to Shaun. The floor of the van was hard, but she grabbed her book bag to use as a pillow. Namia had drifted off to sleep after 10 minutes or so, but awoke between each sleep cycle, listening for her normal sounds, which were not there.

Now that there was some morning light, Shaun was checking his cameras and equipment. Nothing was working. Nothing. He reached under the driver's seat and pulled out a leather folio. He opened the flap and tried the pen. The pen worked on the notepad. He showed it to Namia, "My job is to record your interviews and the scenes you report from. I guess I'll have to use this if you want to get to work this morning."

She laughed, "I suppose you're right, if we can't get to the studio easily, we may as well keep working where we are." They rinsed their mouths and splashed their faces with the water they had with them and headed out the van door to be journalists the old-fashioned way.

After a good night's rest, Mari's parents arrived with the four children. After lots of hugs and kisses and good wishes for mother Mari by her children, everyone began loading up last minute stuffed animals, children's books, portable devices, and other favorites from home, while Mari went below for another nap. Then the two men drove in tandem to the car rental office so Jake could drop off the rental car he had rented from Atlanta. It was now about 9 in the morning. He knew they would not push off until noon when they were to rendezvous with Jasmine, if she could make it.

With everyone else aboard *Point of Departure,* Jake drove to a moderately used part of the grass parking lot and found a place to leave the family minivan. He pulled some pavers out of the hatch and placed them immediately in front of all four tires. Then he drove the tires up onto the pavers. Once the van was properly parked, he reached under the hood and disconnected the battery. He added a quart of Stabyl in the full fuel tank. He rechecked the interior for any last minute items that were needed. Then he pulled a cover from the hatch, locked the vehicle, and covered it with a custom car-cover. Satisfied it was secured as well as possible, he shoved the keys into his pocket and walked toward the docks. He turned and snapped a photo of the van, in its relative location, in case it was missing when they returned.

Jake joined the rest of his family on board. The kids played a quiet game of jacks on the berth next to Mari, while the rest finished stowing the toys, books, and gear. Mari's mother served some pineapple chunks and crackers. And they sat and watched the clock hoping Jazz would join them. They didn't expect her to, but they had promised to at least wait until noon. Mari decided to call and text Jazz one last time at 11:00 a.m. but the phone rolled over to voice mail and there was no response. She decided not to worry about her sister. There was nothing she could do now. She sensed that Jazz was fine, though still contending with her whirlwind trip to Virginia.

SEVENTEEN

Tuesday Morning, The White House

Bella awoke suddenly, exhausted from just a few hours sleep. She was on the sofa in her office. She threw her legs around, popped up off the sofa, darted to her desk and checked herself in the mirror she kept in her desk drawer. After a touch up under the eyes to rid herself of smudged makeup, she reached into another drawer and pulled out her mouthwash, taking a swish, and spitting into her trashcan. She reached for the phone, but it was still dead. She looked on her desk at her fried cell phone and dropped it in disgust. She looked out the window and saw crowds of people milling about outside the gates. She shook her head at her helplessness. Then she went out her door and down the hall toward the Station.

The hallway was dark without electric lights. At the far end a candle burned in an old-fashioned hurricane lamp. She reached the desk and asked the secret service agents if there was any news from the outside. Hearing her voice, Weatherby stepped out of the adjacent office and gave Bella a long, silent look.

She followed him into his dark office for it had no windows. He had a candle half burned down on a dish on his desk while his emergency supply kit lay wide open on the chair next to him, all pulled apart and ready for access.

"Bella, how did you sleep?"

"I collapsed 3 hours ago and scared myself awake. Have you slept yet?"

"Yeah, I took a turn about the same time you did. Manning kept the helm for me while I rested and he's resting now."

"Any changes from a few hours ago? Anything learned?"

"The team we sent out at midnight conducted their recon and to our best estimate, the city was hit by an EMP. That team came back and we assembled another team to find out where the border is of the outage. Most went on foot while Recon 2 left on bicycles. No one has returned yet. We have to assume that means one of three things: they haven't found the perimeter of the outage yet, or they've been compromised, or they are unable to get out there."

"What do you mean they can't get out there?"

"I mean that the crowds and mobs are so large, they might not be able to pass through on the roads."

"Even on bicycles?"

"Well I agree it's unlikely but we were trying to identify all possibilities. Frankly, I was expecting to hear back from someone by now."

"How many did you send out?"

"We sent 7 teams: southwest, west, northwest, north, northeast, east, and southeast. We skipped south since there is no bridge over the Potomac in that direction."

"And no one has returned yet. How long ago?"

"About three hours ago, shortly after Recon 1 returned. But there is another problem."

"Of course," Bella tried to smile at the helplessness.

"Our guard duty around the complex reports that crowds and mobs are growing all around the White House. We don't have enough guards and secret service here to ward them off if they should try to take over. We have plenty of ammunition but not enough shooters. We do not know if this is a plot to take the White House but I would bet that if it were, they would have made a move already."

"You have teams on the roof?"

"Four teams on the corners of the main building and four more teams on the West Wing. Two teams on either end of the tunnel and five teams on the grounds. We also have several 'runners'."

Bella knew that when there were no comms, the runners served this purpose. They would run from team to team in a regular pattern to relay messages in a circular fashion so that the comms functioned, albeit much more slowly than electronic comms. "You mean to tell me we don't have any military-grade EMP-proof comms in house?"

"No, ma'am."

"Well, where are our military? They should know by now we're down and should be here flying us out and establishing a new base of operations!"

"Well, it's possible they were hit, too. Our southeast recon team is heading that way as we speak. They're on bicycles."

"Okay, good."

"Have there been any couriers into the White House?"

"No, we haven't let anyone in since the ambulances left last evening."

"But what about news of the President?"

"We have no news of the President. I'll let you know if we get any couriers in from the hospital."

"Yeah," she wasn't listening at that moment.

"Bella, if the city was hit with an EMP that means his life support is most likely not working."

"Yeah," she turned and left but to where she did not know.

* * * * *

Alice was pounding on her door demanding entry. Bella dried her eyes. She had taken the last fifteen minutes for crying and reflection. That would be all she would mourn for Perc, though. She opened the door and Alice was taken aback. The look of bewildered sympathy lasted only a moment before Alice barked, "Get a grip, Bella."

"I'm fine, really. Just sleep-deprived and annoyed that this enormous team of experts did not prepare for a triple-header of poisoning, EMP, and civil unrest all in one 24 hour period."

"Hmmphh. So what have your experts figured out for us next?"

"Well, there are three primary directives: restore a functioning government, restore order, and then hunt down these treasonous enemies and bring them to justice. So far, we can't provide a functioning government."

"Well, we're here. *I'm* here."

"Alice, I know you think a lot of your position, but one person does not a government make."

Alice frowned. She trilled her fingers across the desk with an expectant look.

"Look, none of us at the White House can communicate with the military, State, the FBI, the Treasury, DHS, or anyone that takes direction and receives oversight from us. They can continue to their best ability but sooner or later we need *coordination*. Which means we need communications. Once we have coordination, we need access to Congress. Right now we don't know where any of the members of Congress are located. We don't know if we can even convene."

"What about the President?"

"Well, it looks like you'll need to be *installed*. However, we don't have enough officers here to bring a declaration to the Speaker and President Pro Tempore. So you *cannot* be installed.

"What's the point of being Vice President?" she mumbled to herself as she got up to leave Bella's office. At the door she asked, "Are they coming for us?"

Bella looked up in surprise. Was Alice referring to the military or the mobs? "The recon team from the Pentagon returned a few minutes ago and said we should be out of here later today. You'll go first, naturally."

Alice stared through Bella, "Good."

The chopper descended on the White House lawn. Alice Bergurner and Ricardo were led by two Marines across the White House lawn to be taken from the White House first. With them were two other staffers. Bella watched their departure from the window with trepidation. Weatherby had walked up beside her to watch, too, "Where are they taking her?"

"To Andrews for now. They have a command station established where we will all rendezvous. Here is the list of departures to evacuate all of us. Sorry, Weatherby, but you are on the last chopper out of here."

"That's all right, ma'am."

They watched in silence as Alice, Ricardo and the others were strapped into the chopper. The mobs behind the fence lurched forward and a moment later a swarm of ant-sized men piled across the fence and approached the rear of the helicopter near the tail rotor. "Oh, no," Bella uttered. There were close to 40 men now, moving closer to the rear of the chopper. Now the Marines on the ground were waving the pilot to get airborne as quickly as possible as they drew their firearms. Bella and Weatherby both stared out the window, paralyzed by the inability to do anything nor quickly enough. The mob of men had thrown a cable of long length over the tail fin of the helicopter. The path of the cable was connected to the gate that the crowds were still held to. A spray of bullets hit the mob near the tail rotor. Two people were spliced as the pilot lifted up and off, others were holding fast to door handles and the tail boom weighing down the port side. As the chopper reached higher, the tension on the cable snapped taught, and the helicopter was swung violently forward then back to the ground. It struck sidelong crushing the hangers-on, and gouging the ground with the main rotor. The cable caught in its force upward, and at that moment the fence yanked loose and the hoard of people pushed through into the grounds surrounding the White House. The sharpshooters on the roof started firing into the crowd as the helicopter's fuel sprang loose and ignited, sending shrapnel and body parts across the browned grass and through the crowd. The mob momentarily retreated in the flash of heat and light. But like ants temporarily thwarted by an obstruction, took to paths on either side of the helicopter and stormed the door of the White House, pounding on the laminated, pressure-reinforced glass in thick, steel, white-washed wood-looking frames. It would hold for a while longer. But how would the remaining helicopters come in?

The Secret Service surrounded Bella, though she could not see where they were going. The leaders had night vision goggles affixed to their faces, they were walking in a formation of sorts, climbing a central staircase. A deafening sound was growing louder. She could hear but not see. It was completely dark. With the exhaustion from lack of sleep and a lack of normalcy, she was now experiencing out-of-body sensations: detachment is the technical term. Her senses were not working properly – at least the perception part in the brain. It isn't *normal* to not be able to see. It isn't *normal* to have so much stress for so long. In her career she had seen a lot, but nothing like the terror of this day.

After she witnessed Alice's helicopter hit the ground and explode, she recalled all the monitoring of special operations she had done over the years. Without the sound, the smell, the intense light, heat, and experience, it is easy to remove oneself from the intensity of feelings that the people on the ground experience. She tried to imagine that. But this was so different. In all those cases the good guys won and the bad guys were served justice for their misdeeds. This time her countrymen were attacking the very symbols of the country. Even if she could imagine that the good guys simply lost a helicopter and a few key people, these people were not real enemies. But what was wrong with them?

She heard a voice beside her, "Ma'am, the chopper is approaching quickly. In a moment, we'll bring you outside, on the roof of the White House, and load you inside. It's nighttime and dark out, so just let us guide you on board. They'll take you away where you will be safe."

"But how are we going to know what's happening here?"

"Ma'am, we have that covered. They're bringing radios and a few hundred pounds of supplies."

A moment later the door blew open and there was a spotlight shining perpendicular to their approach. It was hovering, not landing on the surface. She felt the strong hands on her two arms lift her up and out the doorway and mostly carry her to the cabin door. She shouted, "Thanks, gentlemen," though she couldn't tell whether they heard her.

As she stepped in a hand grabbed hers and vigorously directed her body into her seat and strapped her into the seat's harness. She heard the clicks of other harnesses but her brain wasn't really engaged on the moment – a sort of defense mechanism for the overload. She took a few deep breaths and willed the pins and needles out of her hands and arms and for her heart to slow down. She felt like she only just opened her eyes and saw that there was a full crowd around her of senior staff, including Rebecca.

Suddenly the aircraft swung forward in a leap and swung out over the edge of the building. Bella's curiosity grabbed at her and she stared out the windows. The copilot was shining the spotlight down and around and there were throngs of people on the lawn still banging on the windows. She saw them with a light pole from the Avenue and they were preparing to ram it in one of the lower windows, "God help us."

While flying east for several minutes they passed the Capitol building and saw the West lawn filled with people. "Why are all these people in the streets?"

"Ma'am, as best we can tell they have no water. The city's water supply was completely shut down with the power surge. There is no electricity for heat and lights. We haven't gotten any specific word about what's happening on the ground. It's been about 24 hours. We surmise there has been extensive looting, violent crime sprees, and little police effectiveness. The entire city was grounded to a halt with the power surge."

"Power surge?"

"Yes, possibly an EMP."

"Who's restoring governance?"

Now the co-pilot, who was listening to this conversation, turned around and handed Bella a folio, "Madame Secretary, as the senior-most official available, we need your permission for the Defense department to use its resources to restore order, restore services, and operate the local government until such time as the District's Mayor, Council, and Congress can resume their duties."

Bella took the folio from him. She read the prepared order. She crossed a few phrases and sentences out, initialed them, and then signed the bottom. She handed it back to him. He glanced at the changes and then got on his radio, "We're a go! Repeat, we're a go for Restoring Order."

In a matter of seconds, Bella looked ahead and in the sky were dozens of helicopters coming toward the city from Andrews Air Force Base in nearby Maryland. She heard the roar of fighters above them. As their helicopter descended moving closer to Maryland's border, she saw tanks rolling in to the city. They were followed by a convoy of tractor-trailers.

The copilot looked back at Bella and her study of the vehicles below, given light from her helicopter, and he explained, "Those are water trucks with an attachment of security. We have trucks with lights, power generators, and security teams. We're bringing in communications, too. After we secure neighborhoods, one block at a time, we'll provide water and food for people. Later we'll bring in companies to make repairs to the equipment. This is going to take a long time. Months at a minimum, years more likely. Individuals will have to reach their insurance companies to see if they have coverage. A team will be sent in to investigate whether this was accidental or terrorism."

"What are the implications?"

"I don't know, ma'am, we haven't worked that yet. We've been focused on security for the area first. After all we are still just evacuating you and the others."

"You'd think that people would be prepared for a few days without water and electricity. Haven't we had enough severe storms for people to recognize that that possibility is always there? Or have our providers of water, power, and communications become soooo reliable that people expect perfection always?"

She shook her head, closed her mouth and her eyes, put her head back on the headrest, just to rest for a moment, and was asleep.

EIGHTEEN
Thursday, The Bahamas

The children were still sleeping. Jake and Mari were each enjoying a cup of coffee from the flybridge of *Point of Departure* moored in a large cove of a small island in the Bahamas. They had spent 2 nights there and were now ready to head to West End, Grand Bahama, go through customs, get fuel and provisions, and register their presence to camp by these remote islands for a week or two, on vacation.

When they had pulled away from their dock at Salty's at noon on Tuesday, they had made it smoothly motoring over to the Bahamas. They had enjoyed the dolphins along the way that made part of the journey with them. The kids had fun from the stern snapping photos and tossing extra pineapple chunks. They had arrived by dinnertime and moored in a cove they had visited many times before. Grandpapa and the boys collected firewood and coconuts. That night the family enjoyed dinner and a campfire on the beach before retiring to the cabin to sleep.

They had spent all day Wednesday in their cove. The kids looked for seashells and Jake went fishing. This was a normal experience for them as the family had taken many weekend trips here to go shelling and fishing before. Mari rested but also moved about the cabin for some mild exercise. Nana and Grandpapa searched for some edible berries and nuts on the island. By the end of Wednesday, Mari's strength was much improved and Jake was ready to register their presence with the Bahamian government. He was also interested in getting news.

It was still dark but he yanked open the refrigerator and retrieved the orange juice. It had warmed since the power had been out for about 2 days. He drank it anyway. He climbed on the treadmill, but without power the belt did not advance. He moved to the leather sofa and ritualistically pressed the buttons on the television remote control. As it was the last few times this maneuver was tried, nothing happened in response. He dropped the remote next to him and shook his head side to side. 'What the hell?,' he wondered.

He was unable to reach any of his 45 cohorts. He was unable to get the news. He felt isolated. He never got a clear picture of what transpired with Roullin to know whether the President succumbed to the Negative 1 plan. He hadn't heard from Roullin since he left the White House. He didn't have any idea whether the Vice President was installed. He didn't know what his team had ordered or not yet ordered as of 2 days ago. His food supply was dwindling; his car didn't work; there was no pressure in the water supply; and knowing what was out there, he was not about to leave his fortress. He pulled out his Taurus Model 111 9mm and checked to make sure it was loaded again. Then he re-holstered it. He glanced down the hallway toward the front door where his Remington 870 shotgun was loaded and waiting in the umbrella stand near it.

A moment later the doorbell rang. Kale sprung from his sofa and eased his way down the hall, gripping the stock of the shotgun with a strong hand and gliding toward the front door. Despite the eerie state of his world the past two days, it had been quiet in his neighborhood and in his home west of Georgetown. As he approached the door he could see a single figure in the beveled leaded glass of the decorative door and a large white envelope near its surface. He set the shotgun down next to his left foot, barrel down, as he opened the door on his right side with his right hand. He leaned his face out.

"Mr. Kale Evans?"

"Yes?"

"Special delivery from Baltimore, Maryland."

Kale looked past the young man and saw a van in his driveway with the logo, 'Jamestown Courier Services', "Thank you."

The young man handed the envelope to Kale and stood at attention facing him. Kale looked down at his hand and muttered, "Uh, just a moment."

He shut the door and reached to a bowl he kept on the console table and grabbed one 5 dollar bill. He moved back to the door and handed it out, barely opening the door wide enough to do so.

"Thanks!" the deliveryman called back.

Kale bolted the door and returned to his leather sofa in his office mid-way down the hall to one side. He opened the puffy envelope and found a cell phone, a handwritten note, and a typed letter inside. He started with the typed letter,

"To Mr. Kale Evans: Our apologies that your phone service has been temporarily disconnected. Enclosed is a replacement phone, which we ask you to use in its stead until we can repair damage caused to the telecommunications systems in the District of Columbia following an accident at our central office with a failure in the electrical backup system."

Kale pulled out the handwritten note, "Call the number under 'ICE' immediately upon receipt."

Kale flipped the phone open and scrolled through the list of entries. There were entries for the phone company and its business partners pre-programmed into the phone. Then, under 'I' was the listing 'ICE' for 'in case of emergency'. Kale pressed the send button after highlighting 'ICE' in the phone list.

It rang. And rang. And rang once more. On the fourth ring, there was a woman's voice, "Yes?"

"This is Kale Evans. I just received this phone via courier and an enclosed note requested that I call this number."

"Of course."

Then it was quiet. For a long time. Kale grew impatient. And irritated. But he didn't react because he had nowhere to go, nothing to do, no one to talk with; he was *powerless*.

Then he heard the familiar voice, "What the hell are you doin', Kale? Gee-zuz H. Key-Rist."

"Mr. Star, is that you?"

"Of course, it's me. Who the hell else would pay a courier to drive 50 miles from Baltimore, Maryland to bring you a freakin' cell phone?"

"Only you," Kale was fuming now as he murmured this.

"Look, you dumb prick. I don't pay you to wreck this country. I pay you to fix this country. How the hell does this fix the country?"

"Sir, I had nothing to do with this."

"The hell you didn't. Obviously some rogue person in your *consortium* went for the calamity," he sneered.

"No, I assure you, no one in our organization did this. No one. This was someone else's gig," he paused a long time, "Was it someone on your end?"

"Of course not, you idiot! I only hire loyal people that understand the meaning of coordination and working together toward our common work."

"Then there is another malcontent among us. But whom? Where?"

"Go find out."

"I can't find out. I have no phones, no cars, no news, no computer, no Internet, **nothing,**" he spat it out from frustration.

"Right. Well, use the phone I sent you to try and figure it out. Get yourself out of the capital. Everywhere else is okay right now. Only D.C. got hit. New York is fine. Come up here and use my office if you want to connect with your team and get this resolved."

"I don't have a car. I can't go on foot because there is mayhem out there."

"Yeah, there is. You want me to send a car?"

"Yes. Yes. I'll be packed and ready in an hour. I'll come up there," Kale loved New York. He was suddenly feeling better, more empowered, back in command.

"Okay. Look for it later today. I'll do my best."

The sparkles dazzled as the sun struck the tiny wavelets on the mostly smooth surface of the ocean. The sky was a florescent blue – a solid, flawless glowing umbrella. The light breeze tussled hair. The sea gulls flew closer and closer for a better look at them. Without clouds as a backdrop, the birds controlled the sky.

Ray swept past Jasmine with a "Good morning" even though it was almost noon. She was laundering their clothes in the bait well and said 'Mornin' over her shoulder. Ray climbed up the ladder to the flybridge. He and J.B. conferred for a moment and took turns browsing ahead with the binoculars.

After a few minutes, J.B. readied himself to climb down the ladder. As he did so, he looked down over the edge of the flybridge at Jasmine, 7 feet directly below him; she was only wearing her panties and bra, as she leaned over the tub to wash her clothes and their shirts. He took a moment to admire her slim figure and pale skin. Her hair was in a ponytail and was a perfect backdrop for her smooth skin on her oval face.

"Jazz, what a good morning. You look well."

"I am," she turned to give him a hug.

"It's my shift to sleep, you know. Shouldn't you be resting, too, for the evening shift?"

"Yes, but I wanted to jot some things down and give Ray more information on how to reach Mari and Jake. I'm writing in a makeshift journal that we are distilling our own water, that we're laundering our clothes in bait well, which fish we've caught, cleaned and eaten, that sort of thing." She was using an unneeded boater's manual Ray had on board to do her journaling.

"Well, if you are done with the laundry and your journal before I fall asleep, you're welcome to rest with me."

She smiled. She was ready to take their relationship to the next level, especially since this time in close quarters proved to her that they could get along in any situation. But she kept her distance from him as a show of respect for how awkward it would otherwise be for Ray, on his ship. "Thanks for the offer, but my shift starts in a few hours and I won't be done with this by then," as she waved her arm over all the chores she had in process. He stepped into the cabin disappointed but still confident.

After the laundry was all squeezed damp and hung on the line to dry, Jasmine headed up the ladder to talk with Ray about stopping in at Mari's marina before crossing the Atlantic to head to the Bahamas. Ray had only made that trip once before. He wanted to check on-shore about weather conditions before they made the cross. He looked up at her as she bent over to sit down at his side. "If it gets any hotter here in Florida, we may have to stop for a swim in the cold ocean," he blurted, not knowing what else to say to her choice of garments.

Realizing he was referring to her showing skin, "I'm washing our clothes as well as staying cool," she shared defensively, then changing the subject, "So we should be at their marina in less than an hour. I need to visit their locker."

"It should be less than an hour. I'll refuel, have the black and gray tanks dumped and the fresh tanks filled, plus we can purchase more rations. I figure it will take at least an hour to do all that. Are you going to buy some more clothes, too?"

"They don't have anything there except maybe some beach towels and t-shirts."

"Well, I think it will help me if you wear more clothes around here, okay?"

"Yes, sir. I'll go get dressed now." She had only the clothes on her back when they left the limo in Alexandria. Here the temperature was in the 80s so a swimsuit would be in order. But she went inside and grabbed Ray's clean undershirt and slipped it on. She went back to the stern and wrote in her journal how many sea gulls she counted this hour. She was taking notes on everything they did and saw.

The sounds were growing louder. Kale kept peeking out the front window. His bags were packed: a large office bag and a small suitcase. His leather jacket was on top of them in the hall near the front door. He had the phone in his left pocket and his piece holstered on his right hip. Kale kept hearing the sounds. It wasn't like anything he ever heard before. He ran his fingers through his medium-length, wavy, grayish-brown hair. He was feeling nervous. He was in shape and he was practiced at firearms use. But he knew that mobs were on the loose. *His* operatives must have dispatched them. But they didn't know not to attack *him*. He was supposed to be gone by now. Not here for 2 days. And certainly not with the power and the phones down.

He ran his fingers through his hair again. He pulled the phone out of his pocket. No one had called. No messages. Where was the car that Star was sending?

He paced back to the kitchen in the back of the house and grabbed a warm can of Coke. He drank a swig and spit it out in the sink. There was no water and there was nothing cold. He paced back to the front of the house. He glanced at the phone again. Then he ran his fingers through his hair. It felt a bit greasy. There was no water to take a shower. It was two days since he had a shower. He had to get out of here. His anxiety mounted.

He returned down the hall to the kitchen. This time he opened his bag of pretzels and started munching on them. He heard the sounds again. It was a chanting sound. He couldn't tell what they were saying. Then he heard gunshots, which sounded like they were just a couple hundred yards away. *That* was too close. A moment later, he saw people leave the side window of his neighbor's house on the next street, not far from his own back yard. Now he felt ill.

Bang-slam. The sound pounded his ears due to his jitters. A moment later the sound registered in his brain as the doorknocker. After he gathered his wits, he raced down the hall back to the entryway. He could see a figure outside of the beveled glass. *Why had he put in this glass door?* It was just as easy for someone out there to see in. He peaked through and saw it was the driver and his car. He grabbed his bags and jacket and slowly opened the door. The driver had a serious look on his dark face. "Mr. Evans?"

Kale never heard such a deep voice before, "Yes, you're taking me to Baltimore?"

"Dat's da plan. Balti-mer and den da train to New York. Ready?"

"Yes."

The driver reached out to grab Kale's bag. Kale decided to let him take the suitcase while he grabbed his office bag and jacket. After he stepped out the door, Kale turned to lock it.

Then they took the fifty paces to reach the car in the driveway. There, they could hear gunshots from behind the rear of the house. Kale jumped from his skin. The driver scowled and quickened his pace.

The driver's long legs brought him to the car first and he opened the rear door on the passenger side, swung around the rear of the car, threw the suitcase into the trunk while Kale reached the door and climbed in and closed the door himself. The driver was inside an instant later.

Kale felt himself actually breathe. It had seemed he hadn't been breathing for a full minute as they moved from the house to the car. The driver started the car and backed down the driveway. As the car reached the street, a group of six young men were running toward them down Kale's driveway from the side yard. They were yelling and shouting. Kale resisted the natural urge to open the window to hear what they were saying. He resisted his curiosity to find out what would happen next. Instead he slunk down in the back seat. The driver accelerated and squealed the wheels as he shifted the transmission from reverse to drive while still moving with the momentum of the sloped driveway. The young men lost ground as they descended the driveway but gained upon the change in direction of the car. One man jumped onto the hood of the car. Kale yelped and the driver growled.

The driver swung the wheel violently in the opposite direction and the man was losing his grip. Another man jumped on the trunk during this maneuver and Kale yelped again. By now he pulled out his Taurus and aimed it in front of him. The driver shouted, "Don't!"

The man on the hood laughed as he lost his grip and rolled off the hood on the passenger side. Kale could hear him hit the ground through the window. The man on the trunk had little to hold on to. The driver accelerated down the street and then swept the car side to side until his hanger-on fell off, too.

Kale felt a moment of relief. The driver was shaking his head. Kale finally asked, "What the hell is going on out there?"

"Man, we heard in Balti-mer that the power was out in D.C. But they kaint fix it. Too much is broke. We heard it's all under control and peeps don't have to do n-thing, hep is on da way."

"Have you seen any help coming here?"

"Man, I ain't seen n'thin'. I drove in from the west to avoid as much of the city as I could. Went way out of my way. But I wadn't goin' to take any chances."

"Smart man."

"We goin' back dat way now. We'll be out-a-here and back to normal soon 'nuff."

Kale sat back and relaxed. He pulled open the built-in drink chiller and found 4 bottles of water, a mini bottle of white wine, and 3 cans of diet coke. Kale grabbed a water bottle and drank it down. He kept looking out the windows for more mayhem. It was quiet as they drove out of his neighborhood.

NINETEEN

Thursday Midday, Indian River Lagoon, Florida

Her clothes were crunchy and stiff from the salt spray and inability to rinse the soap from them. But she felt exhilarated, nevertheless, with the sun, warm weather, fresh air, and serenity of calm seas. She threw the stern line while J.B. threw the bow line to the dockhands at Salty's marina on the Indian River between Cocoa and Melbourne, Florida. Jasmine looked at the people working here. They looked so normal. People were working on their boats, loading or unloading their gear. Everywhere she looked, life seemed to be normal, as though there was no fire and no problem in the Nation's capital.

She stepped ashore and headed for the dock where Mari and Jake kept *Point of Departure* and saw their slip was vacant. She stepped up to the giant footlocker at the end of their slip and pressed the sequence of buttons to open the combination lock. It opened. Inside was the regular gear: hoses, ropes, life jackets, and more, but at the bottom was a large black lock box. She picked it up, closed the locker, and headed back to *Patriot*. Once on board, she opened the box insider her berth and pulled out some cash. She left the box locked under her berth and went ashore again. She found a swimsuit she could wear, two oversized T-shirts, and a beach towel. She bought two chocolate candy bars and went to work on the first one, saving the other one for later.

She saw J.B. heading back to *Patriot* with two full grocery bags and a dockhand behind him carrying two more bags. Jasmine bought two different newspapers and told the clerk they had been at sea for 3 days and wanted to know what was new. The clerk waved off Jasmine with a dismissal, "Not much".

Jasmine pressed some more, "Wasn't there a big fire in D.C.?"

The clerk gave Jasmine a vacant look, "Not that I heard."

Jasmine was perplexed, "Oh, okay, thanks. The guys that told us must have been pulling our chain."

The clerk replied as Jazz was halfway out the door, "Yanked. *Yanked* your chain or *pulled* your leg."

Jazz rolled her eyes. She never could repeat those colloquialisms.

Jasmine headed back to *Patriot* down the long wooden dock. Along the way, she passed Ray. He was done getting fuel and the dockhands were now pumping and filling tanks under J.B.'s supervision. Ray was going ashore to pay for the fuel and to make a few phone calls, since he hadn't been able to reach anyone from his cell phone.

By twenty minutes later the dockhands were done with *Patriot*, J.B. and Jasmine had stowed all the food and supplies, poured themselves instant margaritas from a bottle, and were patiently waiting for their captain to return and give the order to loose the lines.

As they drank their drinks, J.B. started to flirt with Jasmine. She was now at the point where she wanted so much to have some normalcy in life again so they could focus on each other. But they still had to uncover what was happening in the world, in their country, in their capital, and with her family. She stood up suddenly and faced J.B., "Look, I like it when you flirt with me; I want to continue our relationship. But not right now and not right here. Do you understand? I want this problem solved first. I'll have a margarita with you. I'll enjoy fishing and doing the work we need to onboard together. But I can't have us not be focused on solving these problems. We can't be distracted by our attraction to each other. Please, J.B."

"It's killing me, Jazz. What is the use of solving these problems and figuring out how to pick up the pieces of our country, if we don't have a purpose? Right now my purpose is to win your heart, earn your mind, and make a life for us. I already have you pegged, young lady. I'm not going to retreat. I will have you one day and I will keep you. Then I will spend my whole life building our dreams. You and me. I'm ready. I think you're ready. I understand you need more space than *Patriot* can provide. But until we have that space, I want to keep you thinking about the next moment, which will be ours."

The warmth had spread slowly at first from the inside to the edges. As it did, it got so warm it was pure heat. She could feel her skin redden, burn, and then glisten. The warmth of it filled her. It wrapped her. It encased her body. And she felt free. This was love. This was goodness. Her heart was pounding as she tried to find some words. The edges of her mouth twitched as she brought the words up from inside her chest, but her lips held them back and J.B. did not hear her sentiment, "So this is love." She regained some composure and instead teased him about the margaritas, "Say that when you're sober." And they both enjoyed a laugh.

He reached over and gave her a short, soft kiss on the lips. As she sat there quivering and swaying, J.B. stood up and greeted Ray as he returned to *Patriot*. Jasmine looked up at the backside of J.B. and saw him differently now. The air between his back and her eyes was filled with moving energy particles and made her dizzy. She saw how much she was attracted to him. He was man. And she was woman in that moment. She was ready to fall to her knees then and there and serve him as her god. Was that love, she wondered? The two men went up to the bridge to go over weather printouts and charts as she still sat there, unable to move. She realized in the next moment what love was – the infinite desire to give to another anything and everything. Hadn't he just promised the same to her? She saw it now, more clearly as her head started to sort through it. Love was about giving. And this man that had stood before her a few moments ago that she saw anew was perfection *for her*.

Suddenly, she realized, too, that focusing on their problems and solving the problems was not a goal to be achieved in order to tackle the next goal, the next sales goal, the next professional goal, or achievement goal, but rather a process of living and through that process having a partner to work with steadily side by side. She was now able to see as J.B. was seeing.

Ray interrupted her thoughts, "Jasmine, aren't you coming up here?"

"What? Oh, you want me there, too?"

"Yes, didn't you hear me when I came on board? I have some interesting news."

Jasmine could not ever remember having a lapse of reality before. She chuckled to herself and allowed herself to revel in her humanity, that love conquers even her. She was beaming.

"Did you get some good news from the clerk?" Ray was looking at her stare blankly back at him. Then turning to J.B., "How many cocktails did you two have?"

"I'm fine, Ray. She had no idea what I was talking about. It seems that any news from the Capital never reached this part of Florida."

"That seems so unlikely."

"I bought these two newspapers. The *Sun-Sentinel*, which is Florida-wide and *USA Today*." Jasmine started thumbing through the *Sun-Sentinel* after handing the *USA Today* to Ray.

It didn't take long to browse the thin newspapers. "Nothing in here," Ray responded with total puzzlement.

"Here's something," said Jasmine, "It says that since the Nation's capital is on temporary shutdown, Florida's legislature is convening starting on Monday. 'Governor Harris has called a special session of the Florida legislature to convene beginning on Monday citing the Federal government shutdown of earlier this week. Governor Harris is asking the State Legislature to write a bill to authorize all federal taxes to be forwarded to the State's Finance Director including income taxes, capital gains taxes, social security and Medicare withholdings, corporate income, excise and fuel taxes, and other taxes ordinarily collected by the Federal government. The revenues will be put into an escrow account from which normal expenses the Federal government returns to the State will be managed and conducted by the Finance Director instead until further notice. This action is similar to that already taken in Indiana, Texas, Alaska, and Wyoming so far. Virginia, Wisconsin, Ohio, and Colorado have also called special sessions this coming week to do the same.'"

J.B. interjected, "What about all your phone calls, Ray?"

"I still couldn't reach anyone. The main and private lines of my office just keep ringing. The main House phone number isn't being answered by neither a person nor the answering machine. I've tried to call the cell phone numbers of my staff and they just roll over to their voice mail without ringing. I tried the main numbers of Transportation and no one is there either. The answering machine in my apartment isn't answering. Not even my regular barber. Not my favorite take-out restaurant. No one. It's as if all the phones in D.C. were shut off."

Jasmine sat imagining what it must be like for the people that lived there. Then she looked around her again and thought that these people, here in Florida, seemed better off.

Ray mumbled to himself, "I'll try the DoD next."

J.B. became serious, "I don't think we should go to the Bahamas, Jasmine. I think we should stay here in Florida at least for now, so long as it's functioning, so we can be here to help. I think both Ray and I have a duty to do what we can, as elected representatives of the Congress."

"No argument from me. If we can find a way to my place, you are both welcome to room with me."

"I was thinking more in terms of trying to reach Tallahassee. As elected members of government, I think it makes the most sense to go there and work with the State's elected members of government."

With a look of surprise, Jasmine slowly nodded her head affirmatively, "Ok. I guess I'm along for the ride."

"Uh-oh," the deep voice interrupted the quiet.

Kale was just feeling relaxed, less agitated and serene, now hydrated on plenty of cool water and snacks that were in the car that Star had sent for him. This was all interrupted by the good driver that had rescued him, now showing outward signs of concerns. Kale roused himself from his meditation to look out the window to see what was concerning the driver.

Ahead of the car the street was blocked by a mob of youths of all shades of brown, from the palest-off-white to the deepest ebony and all shades of brown in between. They were all men; young men. Kale could see signs in the hands of some of them as they were marching into the City. The professionally produced signs read, "Time for Change" and "Keep Us Safe" and "Fight for Fairness" and several with a large, surreal clenched fist in deep red shades. Then there were hand-drawn signs calling for "Socialism Now", "Give me the Wealth", "Karl's Komrades", and "F--K Capitalism".

Kale realized that all of the preprinted signs he could see were ones his organizations had produced and distributed at recent events over the past few weeks and months, including the "Keep Us Safe" a week ago and the socialist-fist sign for the event planned two days ago. He sighed. He knew what was coming. He had trained their leaders, after all, on how to motivate the masses. It included targeted violence of the "haves". Right now he was sitting in a nice limousine being driven by a driver. He knew he was exactly the type of target they would pick. He pulled his Taurus out of his holster ready to fight off anyone that got inside the car. "Driver, back up, man!"

"I kaint do dat, suh."

"But they'll kill us both if they can get in the car."

"I show' hope not."

"But look at them! Stop the car!"

The driver stopped. But by now they were just 40 yards from the crowd.

"There's still time to get out of here. Back up and head down a side street!" Kale felt desperate now. He could see people coming through the crowd with metal pipes, machetes, and poles. They were throwing rocks and debris at the car now as they kept walking closer. Kale hadn't felt so powerless but when he was a child. Everyone he paid listened to him and took his orders. Why wouldn't this driver *do* something?

"Mr. Evans. Yo' employer told me dat once I had you in da car, I was to take you to Balti-mer by following dis road. He did not say I should evade mobs of yoots roamin' the neighborhoods. He said I should 'stay the course'".

"But aren't you worried for your *own* safety?"

"Those is my people right der. I ain't worried. You worried?"

"Heck, yeah!"

The driver chuckled as though he just heard a classic joke. Then, as the mob swarmed the vehicle and started pounding the car and its windows, and people were trying to open the doors, the driver pressed the 'unlock' button on his console. Kale had a moment of shock realizing the driver was aiding the mob in what was sure to come next. He felt a hand on his shirt as he looked to his right and a man was yanking him out of the car. He fired a shot and the kid fell into his lap spurting blood on his suit. Others were reaching in on the driver's side and pulling out his office bag and the drinks and snacks. Kale felt a weight lift from his lap as the youth was pulled off by one of the mob. Kale fired another shot at that one and he fell backwards from the force hitting his spine and pushing his body backwards. Kale shoved him out and tried to close the door. As more people shoved into the car from behind the crowd, Kale kept shooting and they kept dropping. He had to lock the doors. He pressed the button when his door was shut but there were three more people in the car —two in the front seat and one next to him. Plus the two doors were open. Kale shot the driver in the back of the head, pressed the 'door lock' button and then shot the guy in the back seat next to him, then shot the two in the seat in front of him. Kale then tried to reach the door next to him to lock it. As he leaned over someone grabbed his arm and pulled on him. He lost control of his body's position so he couldn't pull himself back without putting the gun down. He wasn't going to let go of the gun so he let himself get dragged to that door. He reached out and shot the man yanking his arm and pulled the door closed. It was locked now, too. One more door to go. Two more people climbed into the front seat and were jumping into the back seat with him. They were blocking his way from reaching the last door. One was grabbing his gun. He shot him – that bullet went through the hand. He shot him again. That one hit his hip. He shot again and the windshield got hit. Now members of the mob were dancing on the hood of his car and stomped on the windshield until it fell in. The mob continued to pour into the car. This wounded man finally pulled the gun from Kale's hand and shot him in the chest.

As Kale looked down at his body, he saw the blood pouring out through the hole. But he was still conscious. The pain was not as bad as he thought it would be. It felt like a wasp sting. And a bit wet. He watched the crowd cheering and whooping as they rocked his car and danced on the hood. He could smell an awful smell of filth and sweat and rot. It got worse and worse as he felt his brain starving for oxygen. He felt woozy and drunk. The scene started flickering as his eyes could no longer focus. The smell kept getting worse. He imagined this was Hell. He realized in his impending death that his life hadn't meant anything or any good. Mr. Star had left him to die at his own hands. Why hadn't he spent his life following his own calling, rather than doing Star's bidding? He saw starlight flickers as everything went dark. The sounds faded. And he gasped his dying breath.

The temperature was dropping as the sun moved down her shoulder. Dolphins were swimming alongside *Patriot* and she swore they were smiling at her on purpose. Some sea gulls flew past the stern to find a place in the nearby trees to roost for the evening. The motor was humming along and the wake was lightly splashing itself above the propellers. She didn't notice the sound of it anymore; it was the new normal. Her skin had changed from being in the sun and the wind and the weather so many days. She felt ruddy. She wondered if she could conduct her sales business from a yacht like *Patriot*. Maybe with videoconferencing and some shore visits, she thought. She allowed herself to daydream some more integrating her new reality with her life experience as she went about the chores. Her vegetables were chopped and she was ready to put the lot on the grill with the flatfish that Ray caught earlier in the day.

Over dinner Ray had explained he had reached the Department of Defense; they were functioning normally, without a blip, and would petition the State governments for 30% of the federal taxes they were collecting to be forwarded to the Pentagon Budget Director for administration of National Defense. So far all the States that had convened had agreed to this request. A new day seemed to be dawning over the countryside.

After dinner was finished, Jasmine went to the helm to drive her evening shift while J.B. washed the grill and dishes and cleaned up the galley. Ray had turned in to sleep for a few hours before taking over the night shift. They had worked out a good rotation where they could keep moving around the clock over the past few days and decided to keep up the pace because it would taken another 3 days to reach Tallahassee; they would arrive in time for the opening session on Monday, so long as there were no delays.

The entrance to ECF Studios looked the same as always except the crowd of people lined up on the sidewalk 50 feet away. There were families with small children, elderly people on canes or in wheelchairs, some teenagers in small groups, all waiting patiently. At the front of the line was a large semi with several healthy people wearing red T-shirts with white, square crosses on the back, dashing in and out, handing supplies down to a few more red-shirted young men and women behind a table below the back of the truck. Water bottles and snack packs were being distributed to those who were waiting in line, who were carrying plastic grocery shopping bags to fill.

Shaun and Namia looked on with desire, not having eaten anything but dried potato sticks for two days and using up the water they found along the way. Though exhausted they both ran to the entrance of the studio. Armed guards blocked the locked doors as they approached. Namia had her badge still strung about her neck and showed it to the guard. He pointed to a sign that read, "ECF Employees Only". Shaun announced, "I'm Shaun Davis and this is Namia Pruvati. I'm a cameraman and she's a reporter. We were in the field and have only just found our way back here after being out here for days. We're exhausted but ready to share our reports."

"You'll have to wait. Over there." He pointed to a space on the ground on the sidewalk to the side. There, another guard was watching over one other person. They approached and sat down next to him.

"Hi. What is going on?"

"They only open the door to let us in at times that seem random to all of us, but I guess they're just ensuring no members of the public sneak in."

The door opened behind Namia and another guard stepped out and said, "You three may come with me – quickly."

Shaun was still standing and held a hand out for Namia. She took it as he eased her upright. The other fellow stepped in front of them and they went inside. It was cold inside and eerily quiet.

TWENTY

Friday Morning, ECF Studios, Crystal City, Virginia

Namia awoke with a start. She was sleeping on a sofa in her boss's office. She trotted down the hall to the restroom where put herself together enough to face her co-workers. As she returned down the hall, the producer, Gary, told her she was being assigned to Richmond, where the State Legislature was taking matters into their own hands. She was handed a new laptop, some CDs of ECF's broadcasts for the past 24 hours, and a new cell phone programmed to take calls from her old phone number. She took the gear bag and headed for her workstation, where she kept two spare outfits she could change into. She called back to Gary, "What about wheels? Do you have a vehicle for Shaun and me?"

"Yes," he called back, "the keys are in your bag to one of the vans in the lot. They're still working!"

On Friday morning *Patriot* arrived in Key West for refueling and fresh provisions. While Ray stayed with the yacht, J.B. and Jasmine took a walk north and east from the dock to reach the tourist areas. They bartered to purchase 3 used scooters and 3 spare fuel tanks. They hired a passing teenager to drive the third scooter to *Patriot* for them. After loading the scooters onto the deck above the bow and stowing the fuel tanks in the stern, the three were ready to push off. They were making good time and expected to reach Tallahassee mid-day on Sunday.

Among the provisions Ray purchased were a trio of N.Y. strip steaks and some Idaho potatoes. "I don't know about you two, but while I love eating fish, I also love eating steak."

J.B. responded, "My mouth is watering. What can I do to help prepare dinner?"

Ray handed him the potatoes to slice into wedges and some garlic to mince. Jazz offered to help, too. "No, young lady, you man the helm once we're underway and let us men cook for you tonight," his eyes twinkled as he said this. He was clearly having a grand time on their adventure. He looked back at Key West as they pulled away from the dock and sighed, "I guess the world has changed as we once knew it. The great unknown is up ahead. What awaits us, we shall be patient to discover."

He turned the controls over to her, climbed down and stepped into the galley to collect the marinating steaks as he moved to the stern where the outside grill was preheating. He placed the steaks onto the surface and took the foil-wrapped potatoes from J.B. and placed them alongside the steaks. Some sea gulls began to fly downwind from the grill looking for loose tidbits.

The three of them looked forward to the northwest, to the future. Ray felt unease, J.B. felt an ominous weight ahead, and Jasmine felt the winds shift and grave concern for what was ahead. Then she caught a whiff of dinner cooking and her mind returned to the present, a beautiful moment to sail away.

* * * * *

Jasmine had been sleeping soundly on a full belly of the grilled steak and potatoes. The rolling sea was her new normal. Overnight they had sailed past the Bay of Florida, hugged the marshes of the Everglades, observed the Ten Thousand Islands, admired the wealth of Marco Island, stayed offshore along Naples rather than taking the Intracoastal, went wide up to Sanibel, and reached Longboat Key. They pulled in to refuel early in the morning.

They headed out for the long crossing of Tampa Bay. A storm blew up from the Northeast taking massive quantities of bay water out to the Gulf of Mexico. The stiff waves were knocking the bow back and forth as they tried to cross the current at a 45 degree angle. Ray had taken the helm and had to slow the engines to deal with the back and forth rocking. He saw the rain approaching and called on J.B. to zip the windbreak shut around the flybridge.

Jasmine was unable to fall back asleep in the weather. She brewed a pot of coffee and headed up to join the men, three covered travel mugs in hand. She took in the sight of the approaching weather, "I guess we could not enjoy fair weather the entire time. How bad will it get?"

Ray checked his radar, "I'm hoping we can get across the Bay before that rain hits us," as he pointed to a red blob on the radar screen. He plotted his speed against the approaching storm and decided he would have to take another tack. We're going to turn west and have the wind behind us. We will avoid this thudding chop and replace it with the big swells lifting us up and down, but the wind will help us get out of the Bay faster."

Jasmine climbed down to the main deck and pulled out the three raincoats. She put hers on and handed one to J.B. as he had climbed down with her. He went to the helm on the main deck and called up to Ray, "I got it!"

Ray quickly climbed down the ladder and took the controls back from J.B. The swells made it difficult to move around but they caught up to the rhythm.

Within minutes the rain overtook *Patriot* and the three of them stayed on deck together but J.B. closed up the cabin tightly. Jasmine felt a mix of fear and excitement. She tried to let the fear go knowing odds were still in their favor despite the feeling of being so small next to the storm.

Once they passed Fort DeSoto the sea was much calmer, the wind slowed by the trees and land. As they motored near shore farther along, the rain subsided over them as they watched it to their south still wreaking havoc.

The next few hours they enjoyed the view of the beachfront resorts and the gradual clearing of the weather. The temperature began to drop and Jasmine put on all the clothes she had with her, including the sweatshirt and jackets.

J.B. also put more clothes on to warm up. He came out of his cabin to see Jasmine brewing more coffee. He reached up behind her and hugged her. "I can't wait until our cruise is over and you come live with me."

Jasmine was enjoying the hug and when he said this, she stood still and was unable to respond. J.B. turned her around to face him. "You don't have to say anything," he gave her a kiss. Then he added, "you and me, together," pointing to her then himself, and he stepped away leaving her weak-kneed and delighted.

Jasmine went to the helm to take her turn from Ray. He turned in for his afternoon nap. A moment later, J.B. also turned in. So Jasmine had her thoughts, the helm, and the enormous Gulf of Mexico to think, really think, for the next 4 hours. The autopilot took her past Homosassa and Cedar Key and along the marshy nothingness of the Big Bend of Florida. She thought about her purpose in life, her goals, her values. She weighed her career and her family in the mix. Just days ago J.B. was not a part of any of that. Was there a void and vacuum then that she was aware of? No, not really. Would there be a void and vacuum if he wasn't in her life next week? That was too heavy to ponder. Would she be unhappy if he were not part of her life next week? She was not sure. But she did recognize that she would be happy to have him in her life next week and for the foreseeable future. She remembered his surprise, come-from-behind hug. She *liked* that. She wanted *that* in her life. She wanted his attention and his interest in her.

It was dark now and Ray came to the helm. He told her he was going up to the flybridge to drive and would take the controls there. She handed them off and covered these controls. But before she went to bed for the night, she climbed the ladder to ask Ray about J.B. Had he had any special woman in the time they knew each other? Why not? What drove him? Ray had not given her any clarifying answers except to say that he knew J.B. had gone on several "dates" during the four years they knew each other. Each time it was a different woman. And each time it was for some political event, such as party or charitable fundraisers, invitations to the White House, and other events where it is appropriate to have a date or an escort. Ray also divulged that these women were beautiful or at least held their own. No, Ray never saw any of them twice. No, Ray had never seen J.B. show an interest in them as he had to Jasmine.

"So what does he see in me?" she finally blurted, trying to make sense of what was happening.

Ray laughed at that, "Jasmine, what is love?"

She blinked speechless. Then she thought long and hard about this prospect. She thought about how she felt the last few days. It felt like love. But was it really? Or was it novel infatuation? She certainly liked him. She admired him. She respected him. She decided to climb down the ladder and turn in for the night. Instead of going to her berth, she slipped into J.B.'s berth, which was far too narrow for the two of them. But when he was aware of her presence he rolled to his side and pulled her to him, putting his arm around her and cuddling her. She felt warm and safe. She felt heavenly. This was a wonderful place to be.

TWENTY-ONE

Sunday Afternoon, Apalachee Bay, Florida

Patriot motored into Apalachee Bay over turquoise waters, slowly moved up the Waukulla River to St. Marks where they moored. After refueling and refreshing provisions, unloading trash, and getting the tanks refreshed, they took showers on shore at the marina and rode their scooters the 20 miles trip to the Governor's Square Mall on the edge of Tallahassee. Jasmine purchased a new suit and blouse, several undergarments and new shoes. The men purchased new dress shirts, undershirts, socks, underclothes, and something to wear until their suits were cleaned. They scootered to the Doubletree in downtown Tallahassee where the three of them checked in and arranged for dry-cleaning of their suits to be ready the next morning. After they were all situated they met up in the hotel's restaurant and shared a light meal before moving to the lobby where Ray made two dozen phone calls, J.B. made several calls, and Jasmine tried to reach her family and her boss.

While the men were still making phone calls, Jasmine went into the lounge with a newspaper. She watched the news reports on the big screen TVs. Namia Pruvati was reporting from Richmond, Virginia.

"It's been nearly a week since two major catastrophes struck the Nation's capital. First, we now understand that the city was attacked with an EMP – an electromagnetic pulse 'bomb' that overpowered all electronics, batteries, and power systems within a 5 mile radius of a point of detonation. That point has now been identified as the WDCS radio tower. Investigators found a box attached to the top of the tower that had a chemical-reaction bomb in it that sent an amplified power surge throughout the city. All automobiles in the vicinity were left unusable, all telephones and mobile phones were rendered useless, the phone companies' central office switches were impacted as were the local power transmission lines, causing a blackout throughout the city.

"Immediately after the event, crowds filled the streets of the city. Violence erupted as gangs of looters broke into storefronts stealing and vandalizing property. Residents, unarmed because of years of gun control laws, stayed indoors. Those that ventured outside were robbed or assaulted by the criminal element of the city that's been kept mostly at bay by a strong police presence. Police, however, had no communications, no motorcycles, and no cruisers for the first few hours until word could reach nearby stations to loan some. Police bicycle patrols were attacked by vandals, their bicycles were stolen and they had to retreat to the police station on foot. The Metro is not yet operating and the National Guard has been called in to prevent entry to the city at all points. Roadblocks have been put up everywhere. Additionally, we are hearing reports they are not letting people leave the city until they can verify that they are not lawbreakers running loose in the streets.

"Meanwhile the hospitals' uninterruptable power systems, also known as UPS', were impacted by the EMP as well, resulting in deaths of numerous patients that were relying on dialysis, mechanical ventilators, gastric feeding tube pumps, and artificial external pacemakers for sustained life.

"Now, several days later, here in Richmond, the capital of the Commonwealth of Virginia, the House of Delegates is convening and setting up a special link to other State capitals to convene the Congress via the many States. The Virginia General Assembly passed an emergency order transferring its representation in Congress to itself until the U.S. Capitol is restored to operation, as determined by the Virginia General Assembly. The Governor of Virginia signed that bill this morning.

"We have word from our local affiliates that similar measures are going to be passed in other States this coming week.

"Last week we were also left with the news that our President was in the hospital at the time the EMP was exploded. We have not yet received any word about the President's condition. The White House has been sealed – no one is leaving or entering the compound. Furthermore the Capitol and its office buildings have been evacuated since prior to the EMP because of a bomb scare. Most members of Congress have not returned to the Capitol and those present cannot conduct a session of business until a quorum is reached. The members present have requested that those that left the city convene in State capitals.

"Meanwhile the State capitals are on high alert for more EMP bombs that might be detonated near them, making them incapacitated. Officials have requested that persons disconnect their batteries in their cars when not in use, to shut off circuits on their home and business circuit breakers when not in use, to unplug appliances, pull batteries out of devices when not in use, and to keep spare electronics and appliances available in case another EMP is detonated while they are using their cars, appliances, or electronic devices. This is Namia Pruvati with ECF News, reporting from Richmond, Virginia."

Jasmine pondered this alone, since the men were making phone calls. She reviewed the events of the days since they left the snack bar in the Rayburn building and it made sense, based on what she experienced, but she had no idea this was even a possibility. She put her head in her hands and cried for the innocent people harmed by the ordeal. Even Roman, slain at the hands of the anarchists that took advantage.

The Customs and Immigration government office building in West End epitomized the essence of the Bahamas: it rose above the waterline with colonial style, a bright reddish-pink shellfish hue, and a shaded porch to welcome visitors. The walkway to its entrance was adorned with bougainvillea and firebush, lizards, buntings, and goldfinches. The walkway was a hodgepodge of tile, pebbles, and bricks. The path meandered to a paned glass door, left wide open. The floor was a mix of rustic wood floorboards adjoining spreads of ceramic tiles. The ceiling was lofty, with a dangling ceiling fan whispering in circles. Along the side were several windows wide open to the fresh air and a slight breeze sailed through the space.

Mari and Jake went to the queue in front of a tall counter, behind which were a few locals working the government's concerns. An overweight man with greasy hair sat on a tiny wood chair at the far end of the counter, with a dark blue uniform shirt and matching slacks. He had a bandolier of bullets over his left shoulder and his Colt 45 revolver was hanging from under the same shoulder in a loosely hanging holster.

When it was their turn to approach, Jake stepped forward first and Mari followed in his wake to reach the counter. "Good morning," Jake greeted the young woman with chocolate skin and tight curls around her smoothly etched face.

"Good morning. How may I help?"

"We are visiting the Commonwealth and are here to register."

"Excellent. Please fill out this and this, and then both of you sign here," she efficiently showed the entry form to Jake and gave a welcoming look to Mari while showing her where to sign.

The form was simple and there was no one behind them in the queue, so Jake stayed in his place to complete it, sign it, have Mari sign her place, and hand over their passports.

"Welcome to the Bahamas," she warmly greeted them.

Jake looked over at the guard, who seemed to be asleep with his eyes open.

They stepped back out through the courtyard and the street to the store to get provisions. Once they left the store they headed back to *Point of Departure*. After boarding Jake maneuvered the boat out to cross over to a new cove. Mari put away the provisions and climbed the ladder to join Jake on the flybridge where she pulled out the newspaper she had purchased there.

"Oh my gosh!"

"What? What is it?"

The headline says "D.C. DONE"

"Isn't Jasmine in D.C.?"

"She was when I spoke to her last Monday."

"Tell me what it says!"

"It says, 'Officials in northern Virginia are now confirming that a 6 mile radius of the Nation's capital has been impacted by some sort of electrical problem. The Metro trains, telecommunications, and power distribution system have been affected. These officials said that there are no recorded deaths or injuries as of yet, although the local hospital has seen a small uptick in the number of persons injured at the hand of another: stabbings and gunshot wounds.

'Local officials in several towns in Northern Virginia have not been able to confirm the location of the President or of senior members of Congress. It is presumed they are safe in lockdown until power can be restored to the city.

'No one has claimed responsibility for the systems failures. One local scientist, who asked to remain anonymous, said it was possible this was a deliberate attack rather than some accidental power surge from the local power company, PEPCO.

'Power company officials were unavailable to comment at this time.'"

"Well, for all our preparations, I can't say that was a scenario I imagined. How much traffic do you think we will run into here over the coming days?"

"There are a lot of Washington beltway types with yachts that would love to live aboard for a week or two while power is restored. I expect we'll have company in the next days."

"Let's go dig up our cache, okay?"

"Sure."

Mari and Jake motored their boat to a tiny sand-bar of an island several miles from the main archipelago. They went ashore with a GPS, a map, and two shovels. The little island only had about 2 dozen trees and several more shrubs and was surrounded by white sand and a variety of crabs. Some fiddler crabs scurried into their holes as Mari and Jake moved along their home base.

Between two trees was strung an old, faded, worn rope hammock. They walked five paces west from it and started digging. It took 30 minutes to dig deep enough. The loud clank let Jake know they reached the cache. While Jake moved the sand from around its sides, Mari rigged up a simple pulley and lever system with some boards she fastened together with rope above the hole, fashioning a hoist. Another 10 minutes and they freed the aluminum box from its safe hole, and slowly moved its mass beyond the pressure of gravity several feet up to their level.

Jake opened the combination lock from memory and inside the watertight seam of the door they found hundreds of pounds of small and large caliber rounds. They closed up the box and rolled it across a system of logs to their dinghy. They floated it back to *Point of Departure* and lifted it aboard with their davit. Mari and her Dad returned to fill the hole in with the diggings and destroyed the hoist.

In a matter of minutes they were underway again and returning to their camp some miles away, to the uninhabited island off Grand Bahama. Mari was at the helm while her sons helped Jake and her parents stow the supplies below decks in every free space. Once stowed, Jake pulled out the 50 caliber anti-pirate gun from below the captain's berth and secured it to its mounts on the bow. He covered it with a sunbrella floral umbrella-looking lounger so no one would be awares, including the pirates. The sunbrella had slits for the muzzle and for viewing the surroundings and for access into the hidden space from which the shooter could shoot.

TWENTY-TWO
Monday Morning, Tallahassee, Florida

With fresh business suits, crisp new dress shirts, new razors for clean shaves, both Ray and J.B. were glad the adventure at sea was now over and they could get back to work. Jasmine also felt a sense of femininity and professionalism that had been lost at sea for the last several days of salt spray and bare skin now that she was dressed up and made up. The three walked from the Doubletree toward the Capitol in Tallahassee's center. They walked to the Old Capitol, a stately and beautiful historic building with its period striped awnings over its array of windows. From the north side they took a staircase down, crossed the plaza, and joined the queue to enter the security checkpoint at the new Capitol, a rather drab phallic symbol of 1970s tradition.

After entering the lobby they maneuvered to the bank of elevators and rode up to the fifth floor where they entered the gallery overlooking the House legislative chamber. They were not sure whom to contact to be recognized so they decided to watch the State's business before finding the Sergeant-at-

Arms or the Clerk-of-the-House and join the proceedings on the Floor.

A roll call was just announced for CS HB X1. That must be a committee substitute of bills that the House and Senate had already voted on themselves and now both houses were voting on the reconciled version. J.B. looked around for any papers that would describe the current transaction. In the background, he could hear the names being called, "Adamson", "aye", "Browning", "aye", "Brunacher", "aye", and he stood up and walked over to the nearest person in the gallery, "What are they voting on?"

"CS HB X1," was the response.

"Yes, but what is that CS?"

"Here," she said as she handed him the printed agenda with a summary of the bill.

J.B. scanned it as he returned to his seat next to Ray. It said, "A bill entitled *Emergency Restoration of Governance to the States*; Whereas the U.S. Capitol is and has been incapacitated, whereas members of Congress are not in session and will not be for the foreseeable future, whereas the President of the United States is out of commission, whereas the Vice President of the United States has not been sworn in, whereas many functions of the Federal government are not being provided and must continue, and whereas governance that is local is best, the State of Florida does hereby decree a restoration to the limited form of central governance as founded in 1789 by the U.S. Constitution, limiting Congress' powers to those enumerated in Article One, nullifying several prior U.S. Supreme Court decisions that expanded the powers of Congress beyond those and reduced the powers of the Many States therefrom (listed in Appendix B).

"During the transition phase, from this point forward, all previously required Federal taxes collected by individuals and businesses living, visiting, or conducting business in Florida will be transmitted to the Chief Financial Officer of the State of Florida through the Department of Revenue. Such sums as were previously committed by the Federal Government to the Department of Defense will be forwarded by the Florida CFO to the Under Secretary of Defense Comptroller at the Pentagon in an amount proportional to the number of members in the House of Representatives, per the Union of States agreement of yesterday. Once those funds are deducted, distributions will be made to Florida's Veterans as per prior commitments up to receipts available. Once those funds are deducted the CFO will distribute social security and Medicare checks to Florida's Retirees and Disabled Persons to the extent such funds are available. Until further notice, all other Departments, Agencies, and functions of the Federal government no longer exist. The Federal courts will be disassembled, the Federal law enforcement agencies will be disbanded, Federal Departments of HHS, HUD, Energy, Education, et cetera no longer exist. Excise taxes will be collected by the respective ports by the States in which they reside. Customs agents will be transferred to State employment. Treaties previously adopted will be assigned to the Pentagon for review. Those treaties that address common defense will be reviewed and revised by the Secretary of Defense; all such treaties must be approved by two-thirds of the States. All trade agreements will be transferred to the States from whose Ports of Entry are impacted. States may form consortiums, e.g. Pacific states, Atlantic States, Gulf States, and so forth to negotiate common treaties.

"After the transition period, during the next regular session of the Florida State Legislature, Veterans benefits, Social Security, Medicare, income taxes, FICA taxes and all other prior Federal programs now falling under the State's umbrella will be the States' purview to define, manage, and operate.

"All parts are separable in the event any part is struck down. This bill will become law immediately upon the Governor's signature."

J.B. was shocked. Where had he been the last few days? Was this a revolution? Yes, in the true sense of the word, that is a major and sudden change, it is. But not a bloody revolution. The states did not overthrow anything or anyone. But someone had – someone had made Washington irrelevant overnight by exploding a chemical EMP last Monday night.

Ray turned to J.B. and smiled, "We've been working so hard for years to reduce the size and scope of the Federal government by chipping away at programs only to have them double in size each time we lose power to the other party. Well, here you go. Overnight all the work we've aimed for, *and then some,* done," and he snapped his fingers.

By now the roll call was almost done, "Webster", "aye", "Xiu", "aye", "Zuckerman", "aye". "The ayes have it, 118 to two."

Ray could not contain himself. He stood up and started clapping. People around him in the gallery started clapping. J.B. joined him because it felt like the moment to do so. The Speaker pounded the gavel to no avail. When the members of the House heard the gallery members start clapping, they leaned over and congratulated each other with hugs, handshakes, and cheers, from both sides of the aisle. A leaden cloud had been lifted off the State, the People, and the Nation by the transfer of power and control away from a remote city of life-long elite-minded, busy-body bureaucrats to individuals that have a vested interest in their unique qualities of the state's people and geography.

Mari pulled out her computer terminal, which they kept for configuring their navigation and onboard electronics. She connected its wire to a port on the navigation system. Once she was connected, using a simple browser, she was able to access the World Wide Web through its satellite link. There were no JPEGs or advertisements or pop-up windows. Just basic text. She connected to BlogSpot where she entered the address for messages that she, Jazz, and her parents had established for staying in touch. There she read an entry made just a few hours before.

"TALLAHASSEE, FL - This morning Florida passed the *Emergency Restoration of Governance to the States*, similar to laws passed in many other states which acknowledges that the U.S. Government is not functioning and no date is yet estimated when it will be functioning. There are two dimensions to this. First the Nation's capital was hit by an EMP that destroyed all electrical and telecommunications systems. It may be a full year or two before repairs can be completed, according to early estimates. Second, there is a lack of a quorum in Congress and the White House has been disabled. There are reports that the President and Vice President have fled the country and other reports saying they've been injured. The Pentagon is functioning and has requested the States to take this action until such time as the Executive and Legislative branches of government are restored.

"Florida's new law, signed earlier today, established that Florida will collect and administer all Federal taxes that are taken from and distributed to its citizens. Other states are in the process of completing similar measures.

"J.R. reporting from Florida's capital."

Mari shared the news with Jake. They decided to make way to return home the next morning. That night they enjoyed their last dinner in the Bahamas with fresh grilled and marinated conch, white wine and plantains.

The Capitol plaza had been transformed as crowds of people swelled upon hearing the news. The members of the legislature were celebrating, the lobbyists from the surrounding streets joined in, knowing their importance had doubled by this action, members of the community came to celebrate, too, as their town had a more important role for the people of the State. Family members merged into the mix of people. Local bar and lounge operators threw their wares into cars and carts and brought them to Monroe Street where they sold drinks and snacks to the party-goers. Musicians moved in and set up tip jars and played happy tunes. There were red and white balloons and sparkly decorations hanging from trees, attached to façades, and on the bar carts. The festive nature was something new for this city, where debate and argument were the norms.

After lots of eating and drinking and even some dancing, the hundreds of people were wowed with roman candles and mortars launched from the roof of the Capitol's central tower. Jasmine grabbed her journal, drew a picture, and wrote about what was happening: who, what, when, where, why, and how. She knew this was a major historic moment. She didn't quite grasp it all or understand it all, but she figured her big sister would be thrilled and proud of her for her part and for being here. She was missing her sister now and hoping to hear from her soon.

Cruising, they could make the trip in about 4 hours. They were an hour along early Tuesday morning and dealing with a chop from a cross wind and plowing through as best they could. Spray from the crossing waves lofted aboard so Jake kept the clear vinyl windbreak cover down on the starboard side, which faced the wind. This time of year the weather can be treacherous. He was hoping they could make it home before it got much worse. The radar showed an area of disturbed weather off the east coast of the Mid-Atlantic States moving south. As Jake continued to monitor his heading and handle the helm himself to shift around the cross-breaking waves, he was so focused he hadn't bothered to check aft. A cigarette boat was fast approaching in his wake and he could neither hear nor see it. He wasn't expecting company on a rough-weather-weekday in November. And there were no boats anywhere in his field of view.

A sea gull was blown across his path as he was checking for crumbs and favorite scents emanating from *Point of Departure*. Jake's eye followed the bird as it was lifted aloft on a warm current and then floated down again. As his eye followed the gull, he turned his head enough to see the fast-approaching cigarette boat on his port side crossing his wake to come up alongside. With all the sea for miles around, there was no need to be so close and Jake immediately felt a sense of alarm and panic. He had a rudimentary intercom between the flybridge and the galley and he pressed the button three times in quick succession, the signal for something amiss. He flipped two other switches into their 'on' positions, never having needed either before. Mari alerted the others, all of whom were below, "Mom, Dad, we have company, possible bandits! Man the guns!" Then she checked that her children were in their cabin and told them to stay there and be quiet, as she shut the cabin door.

Mari's parents were comfortable with firearms and both hunted and played cowboy action shooting competition games at their gun club. Mari's Dad pulled out two shotguns from the bench seat he was sitting on and handed one to his wife. Mari was debating whether to go to the bow to the 50 cal. She went forward to her cabin and slowly opened the hatch, directly beneath it. It was covered with the sunbrella so she could climb up and out of the cabin, under the cover, and man the gun if she had to. She waited below the now-opened hatch. She listened.

"Hey, Old Man," called the captain of the cigarette boat.

Jake didn't respond orally, he just nodded his head.

"Hey, we need some help," he smiled a strange-looking grin, teeth awry.

"Not sure I can help. I'm bringing a patient to the mainland to a hospital and cannot stop," Jake had planned this scenario before to prevent the need to stop. He was running at a moderate speed of 20 knots now.

"We need some water. We're dry," the cigarette captain persisted.

"Like I said, can't stop, can't help. If you head back, at a heading of 085, you'll find fresh water at the West End of Grand Bahama."

"Look, man. I'm not asking. I'm tellin' ya. We need water, we need it now, and we're goin' to get it from you."

Jake ignored this. One of the switches he turned on started rolling cameras to record what was happening. He knew from this angle he would have clear images recorded of the cigarette boat and its numbers. He had two handguns on his person, one on his right hip and one over his crotch. He had a shotgun next to the helm. And he had his flare gun with several flares under his seat. He pushed the engine control forward to maximize forward thrust and accelerated to a 25 knot speed. The cigarette boat sped up to match his speed and moved ridiculously close to his port side.

As Jake gained speed, Mari quietly moved up onto the bow under the cover of the sunbrella. She waited to cock the gun, though, because she didn't want to give away her position. She would start shooting as soon as anyone else started shooting.

The two boats continued moving forward in this nerve-wracking proximity for several moments before Jake was getting tired of it. He moved to port ever so slightly to 'push' his aggressive antagonist away.

Its captain responded by swerving away, gaining speed and cutting in front of *Point of Departure*. Jake caught his breathe on visions of wreckage and rescue in the cold, open sea. He thought through the physics of such a collision as the cigarette boat moved across, forward, and then slowed on his starboard side, calculating damage to his own vessel and whether to engage in such a risk.

Mari's parents moved from the sofa to the galley to monitor what was happening outside, not sure where else to be to defend themselves.

The antagonist-captain now slowed and moved aft of *Point of Departure*, as though conducting a survey of its weaknesses, boarding options, and its defenses. So far, only Jake was exposed. But while the cigarette boat was moving behind their stern, Mari took the time to cock the 50 caliber gun and get herself into position so she could fire to port, where she anticipated he would return. Her parents moved out of sight to the forward cabin and Mari's Mom retrieved the RPG gun from under the berth. She brought it aft to just inside the main cabin, awaiting a signal.

The cigarette boat emitted three men from its cabin below its helm. They were waving small caliber rifles and handguns at Jake. Jake steered right evading their threat and putting some distance between them. The waves at this angle crashed harder over the starboard gunwale. Shots were fired by the antagonists in a random manner, whizzing past *Point of Departure* and not hitting any part of her great size. That was the signal, and Mari opened fire first, ready for this moment. For her first shot, she targeted the captain at the helm. It missed but by just inches and shattered the windshield into a sparkling array of pieces which by slow motion fell about the helm. Her second shot sent one of the three crew tumbling backwards and overboard without a sign of blood yet visible. By this time her parents were spraying deer shot at the quickly approaching cigarette boat as it seemed their captain aimed to ram *Point of Departure*. One of these sprayed the captain and blood spurted from his neck, arm, and chest. His kill switch engaged and the cigarette boat was left behind in the cavernous wake of *Point of Departure*. Jake knew that another bandit would take the helm any moment. They still had two bad guys to go. Mari couldn't get a shot off now, since she was in the bow and they were aft. But Jake reached into his seat and grabbed the flare gun. He put a mortar-powered flare into the chamber. He waited until the new pilot brought the cigarette boat forward to within 50 yards and he aimed and launched his flare directly at the broken windshield. The flare canister hit the deck and neither bandit seemed to notice, as cigarette boats are exceedingly loud and they may have blinked when the can reached their field of view. There were sights and sounds in succession: first a flash of red light and a bright flash followed by a whizzing sound which was odd and eternal, then a resounding boom of the mortar exploding. Meanwhile the bright flash had spread and there was another explosive sound as the fuel tanks ignited. Bits of colorful fiberglass charred with black carbon filled an ellipsoid path around its point of ignition. After the bits rained down in the sea behind them, as they were still cruising at 25 knots, there was no more threat of bandits and pirates attacking them.

Jake checked his plot and changed his course further south to compensate for the diversion they were forced to take. The waves were not breaking as hard at this angle. The adults agreed to take turns with the binoculars to better monitor their surroundings. The world had changed the past week. Evil-doers were emboldened to engage in carnage, pillage, and wreckage without fear of reprisals.

The steak arrived. It sizzled, dazzled, and aroused her senses. The waiter stood by to make sure she was satisfied. She nodded approval and he stepped away. All three of them were having steak for dinner. J.B. held up his glass of Moragio's Pinot Gris and proposed a toast, "To a New Beginning."

They had been toasting over appetizers and salads already and the wine was going to Jasmine's head. She felt light and alive. She dove into her steak and its bonnets of tomato-mushroom-wine sauce-covered pearl pasta. Her phone rang so she excused herself from the men at the table and walked into the reception area near the entrance, "Hello?"

"Hi Sis!"

"Mari!"

"Where are you and what are you up to?"

"I'm in a fabulous restaurant having a steak dinner with two men in Tallahassee. Where are you and are you better now?"

"We got back yesterday. We've been watching the news ever since we could. You won't believe what we've been through. But we're all fine and we survived. And we hear that the United States is *no* more and the States are all taking all matters into their own hands. This is shocking and unbelievable. And you were in the middle of all of it?"

"Something like that. Here is some better information. You are correct that the Nation's capital is over as we *knew* it. And that the States are taking matters into their own hands. The one exception is the Department of Defense is still functioning. And there is a new President of the United States. Her name is Bella Gliad. She was elected by the new Congress. Since no one knew nor could assemble Congress as it *was*, those that could showed up in Tallahassee or at their own state capitals. Their state legislatures decided whether to swear them in to the First Congress of the Restored Union or not. Most were sworn in over a wide-area networked convention with a new, more substantial oath of office.

"So I've been traveling with two men from the past Congress, J.B. Stanton and Ray Blanzing. I've been with them the last several days traveling from Virginia to Tally. They were sworn in this morning here by their respective States. Legislators that didn't show up in a State capital were replaced by their State's legislatures. So we now have a new Congress with 535 members. They'll be convening in Wichita, Kansas, site of the new temporary capital until they decide whether to move back to D.C. or not.

"With both the President and Vice President casualties of the EMP and ensuing violent uprisings, the Speaker of the House was second-in-line. But he hasn't been found yet. He was last known to be inside the Capitol building when the EMP occurred. So the convention passed a resolution allowing it to name a new President until the next regular election, which won't be for two years from now. Fourth-in-line was Secretary of State Bella Gliad. She was in the Maryland State House in Annapolis all week overseeing the relief effort in D.C., interfacing with the Pentagon, and getting their funding to continue, working with the States, and providing superior leadership. Because she was ranking member of the Administration, she was nominated and unanimously elected to succeed Orinthbey. Then, after being sworn in, she nominated someone from the other party to be her Vice President, something which hasn't been done since Republican Abraham Lincoln's Vice President, Democrat Andrew Johnson. And she was sworn in around noon today. It's a new day and a new world."

"Wow. We'll have to make sure they all stay true to the Bill of Rights," Mari thought out loud. "Does this count as a Revolution? Or is this just a blip in the history books?"

"Don't know. But I can tell you everyone here is celebrating like it's a victory."

"Well, come see me as soon as you can. And when will you be back at work? Your boss called here and left messages the last couple of days."

"I need to find a ride and then I'll be home. Tomorrow. Tonight I'm enjoying my celebration with these men."

"So why do you have *two* men?"

"We spent several days together on Blanzing's yacht. The other one, Stanton, is *special*."

"No wonder you're not back here yet," Mari laughed, "about time you thought about having a special man in your life."

"Yes, well, he'll be moving to Wichita for a time."

"Then I guess you better upgrade your pilot's license so you can fly small jets there and back, hmmm?"

219

After ending their conversation, Jasmine returned to the table feeling happy and confident. As she approached the table, J.B. turned to see her approach and admired her legs and her stride. As she reached his side she leaned over him and gave him a full frontal kiss. He had wrapped his arm around her legs in response. She sat back down and went back to work on her dinner without a word.

EPILOGUE

The sound of voices reverberating around the enormous arched ceilings was loud but distant. Squeals of brakes from trains rumbling along the tracks interrupted the din. People milled about in an apparent random pattern, each with his own destination in mind. Some were fashionable, others distasteful. Rocky awaited his guest at the bar, with the soaring marble wall echoing the adjacent chamber. His cocktail warmed his body while his soul was at peace. He turned toward the enormous American flag suspended from the wall across the chamber and saluted it a moment to himself. He was brought back to the moment when a firm pat was made upon his back. He turned to see his old friend and antagonist, Juan Morovis de Estrella, also known as Mr. Star.

"Rocky!"

"Star. Would you like to join me at the bar or shall we get our table?"

"This is fine. Waiter! Menus and I'll have what he's having," pointing to Rocky's martini.

"So, is our bet over? The States have ended the Federal government, limited spending, and refreshed our Republic. The overbearing, strong, centralized government is no more."

"This is true. However, the social programs, the entitlements are still in place."

"But the States that want less of that will reduce them. They won't increase them because they now have to pay for them directly. Alaska and Virginia can no longer depend on Nevada and New Hampshire to redistribute tax dollars their way."

"Agreed. Look, I concede. Besides I'm done with this game. I've come to a realization. I've lived my whole life benefiting from the free market system. And when I witnessed the carnage and destruction by people we have tried to help all these years in the aftermath of the EMP, I realized our experiment was flawed. Individual people need the ability to defend themselves and choose their paths for themselves, pay the consequences for crimes against their neighbors and reap the rewards of their hard work. Did I tell you they found my Kale murdered in his car?"

"He was like a son to you, wasn't he?"

"Yes, he was with me since the beginning. I was so proud of his work and never told him so. I left him to his own devices that day. I was so furious with him because I thought he betrayed me and launched that thing himself."

"The investigators still haven't solved this. They don't know who set the chemical bomb that night nor whether it was a lone operator or a group."

"Maybe there are others like us, betting society will turn this way or that and then using their influence to direct it this way or that."

"You really have had a 'Come to Jesus' moment, haven't you?"

"Yes, I suppose I have. I don't have much time left on this earth. I'm cashing everything in, moving to the Caymans and spending my last time on earth down there surrounded by a staff that will care for me. I have nothing left without Kale and without our competition."

"Look. I don't need anything from you. Back then, $10,000 seemed like a lot. If you really want to pay up, just donate it to my favorite charity, the UNCF. An educated public and all that."

"Sure. I'll do that. And I'll buy lunch here. Did you know this place, Cipriani Dolci is my favorite?" Star waved his arm around as he said this.

"Yes, I did. That's why I picked it. I'll buy today, too." He could afford to be conciliatory. He had won an enormous success for his country.

"You've always been a good person with a good heart. People have always loved you. I have always envied that."

"It's not too late to start a family, you know," Rocky was starting to feel sorry for Star now that Star was feeling regret and remorse. Never before. He had always been a self-centered megalomaniac without a concern for anyone.

"I suppose. I don't know where to begin."

"Start with a smile and lighten your heart. Maybe you should go to church, too."

They finished their lunch and parted ways for the last time. Rocky stayed behind and watched the passers-by below as Star walked out to his waiting limo to return to his downtown digs.

Rocky paid the bill, walked down to the level for his train north to Cold Spring. He boarded the train and sat waiting patiently. A moment later a young man walked up and sat in the seat next to him. Rocky kept reading his newspaper while the young fellow spent time checking email on his Smartphone. The newspaper article continued to report that there were no leads, no physical evidence, and no indications of whom might have committed the EMP attack. The only evidence they had was a completely melted glob of metal at the scene that they weren't even sure was part of the EMP.

Twenty minutes later Rocky noticed the young fellow was gone. He left a thick document in his seat. Rocky read the title and realized this was the fellow whose company Rocky had just invested in. The venture capital brokerage firm connected him with the company that developed new technology to protect against coronal mass ejections and EMPs. What an amazing coincidence.

His phone rang just then. "This is Warton."

"Rocky!"

"Bella! So nice to hear your voice. When can we get together, Sis? Your big brother wants to come check out your new digs and hear all about your new gig, *Madame President*. How did *that* happen?

ABOUT THE AUTHOR

Peri Parks is a pen name for a scientist turned novelist. Peri's favorite medium for communication is the written word: its abstract symbols combine in an orchestra to fill the mind with imagery, emotion, and knowledge while enduring to share with persons not yet born.

Look for the sequel to Reset, coming soon.